DEAD
IN THE
Water

A Scarlet Cove SEASIDE COZY MYSTERY

Agatha Frost
& Evelyn Amber

For questions and comments about this book, please contact pinktreepublishing@gmail.com

www.pinktreepublishing.com
www.agathafrost.com
www.evelynamber.com

Edited by Keri Lierman and Karen Sellers
Proofread by Eve Curwen

ISBN: 9781549677755
Imprint: Independently published

A
Scarlet Cove
SEASIDE COZY MYSTERY

Book One

Prologue

Liz peered through the door window into the interview room. She wondered how early she could leave the party without it coming across as rude.

"There you are!" Miles, Liz's friend, and fellow detective, said as he walked down the pale blue corridor towards her. "I've been looking everywhere for you."

"I just wanted to take everything in," she said, inhaling deeply, a contented smile spreading across her lips. "See the place one last time."

"Had a change of heart?" he asked hopefully as he played with his curly hair in the way he always did. "You're going to be missed around here. We need you."

"You don't need me. You'll get on just fine."

"*I'll* miss you." His cheeks blushed as he stuffed his hands into his pockets and looked at the ground as he drew a circle with the point of his brogues. "You're as good as a detective gets. Don't you think forty-two is a little young to retire?"

"I think it's the perfect time," she said, glancing through the window again as Karen, the desk sergeant, made a pass at Mitchell, a married community support officer. "Considering everything that's happened, this is well overdue."

Miles nodded. He did not argue, and she knew he never would. He knew better than anyone else at the station how difficult the last two years had been. She had tried to hide her grief from her colleagues for the sake of her job, but Miles had been the exception. He always knew which wine to bring around for dinner to get her to open up.

"I got you something," he said, holding his finger up. "Wait here."

Miles slipped into the interview room, the music from the radio leaking out. Liz almost followed him back into her leaving party, but she stopped herself; it would only make it harder to leave.

He returned with a small orange bag, which had a ridiculously large orange bow wrapped around the handles.

"For my firecracker," he said, glancing at her red, frizzy hair. "I was stuck on what to get you until I saw this. It sums you up perfectly. Low maintenance, a little prickly, but gooey and full of the good stuff on the inside."

Liz unravelled the bow and looked down into the bag, laughing at the prickly green thing.

"A cactus," she laughed. "It's perfect."

"Stick it in your new flat," Miles said, smiling softly at her, the sadness obvious in his eyes. "Where are you moving to again?"

"Scarlet Cove," she reminded him. "On the South Coast."

"What's wrong with Manchester? Scarlet Cove

sounds like something out of a movie. Be careful of those small town people. You think it's bad in the city, but I've heard they're even worse down there."

"I think my days of murder and chasing after thugs are well and truly behind me," she said, looking down into the bag again. "And I'm glad of it. Thank you. This really means a lot."

Liz was not much of a hugger and Miles knew that, but she wanted to break her own rules this once. She rigidly wrapped her arms around his shoulders and patted firmly, knowing the gesture alone conveyed how she felt. The fruity scent of her best friend's aftershave tickled her nostrils, almost prompting tears.

"You can drive down anytime you want to see me," Liz reminded him, pulling herself together as she straightened out her uniform. "And there *are* trains. I'm not even leaving the country."

"I know," he said, tears lining the corners of his eyes. "Look at me. I should go back in. They're about to cut the cake. Are you coming?"

"I'll follow you in," she said, dropping the bag to her side. "Thank you, Miles. Thank you for everything."

"You're very welcome, *Detective Elizabeth Jones*," he said with a wink as he pushed on the door. "You better get used to being just '*Liz*' from now on."

The door closed behind Miles, leaving Liz alone in the empty, sterile corridor. She looked down at the cactus, knowing she would like being '*just Liz*' very much.

Deciding she was not in the mood for cake after all, Liz grabbed her small box of things from her office and headed for the front desk. On the way, she made sure to pass the memorial wall. She looked at the most recent addition and smiled at the portrait of the handsome man with the strong jawline. Even now, it still made her stomach flutter.

"Goodbye, Lewis," Liz whispered, kissing her fingers and resting them on his lips. "I promise I'll try and have a good life."

Liz allowed one tear to slip out before quickly wiping it away. Turning on her heels, she straightened her back, and headed for the front door. With her box of memories and her new cactus, she walked into the bright sunlight, ready for her new adventure.

One

"That's the last of it!" The removal man gestured towards his now empty white van, wiping the sweat from his red forehead.

"I can handle the rest," Liz said, pulling the agreed fee from her small black purse. "Thank you."

The plump man climbed back into his van and started the engine. He gave Liz a small nod before setting off and rounding the corner out of view.

Sensing the sweat running down her face, she pulled a small compact from her bag. Her pale eyes stared back at her, looking all the greener thanks to her bright red cheeks. She attempted to smooth down the flyaway hairs that had snuck out of her low-hanging bushy ponytail. Deciding it was a lost cause, she tossed her mirror back into her bag.

Shielding her eyes from the bright morning sun, she looked up at the small flat above a pale green shop, which was to become her new home. She turned and took in her surroundings as the people of Scarlet Cove went about their daily routines. Her flat was in the middle of a small row of businesses facing in towards a stone town square, which appeared to be playing host to a market. There was a bustling pub to her left, with two more rows of businesses boxing them in on either side. Winding streets leaked away from the square, some edging up the steep hill of oddly positioned multi-coloured buildings poking out of the vibrant trees, and some falling down towards the sea. It looked exactly like the beautiful pictures she had fallen in love with.

Liz slid her phone out of her jean's pocket, itching to look at those stunning pictures again, but a small man with a bulbous nose wobbled towards her with a welcoming smile and an outstretched hand.

"You must be Elizabeth!" the elderly man remarked with a chuckle as he beamed up at her. "Bob Slinger is the name. I'm your new landlord."

Bob rocked back and forth, his wide smile growing as though this was the most exciting moment of his life. With his round belly and crimson nose, he looked like a beardless Santa Claus, but his stature reminded Liz more of an elf.

"People call me Liz." She pushed her phone back into her pocket to accept the man's hand. "It's nice to meet you."

To Liz's surprise, the little man had more than a handshake in mind. He yanked her down into a tight hug, his palm heartily slapping her back. Liz was taller than most women, but her new landlord made her feel like a giant.

"Welcome to Scarlet Cove!" he cried in her ear as he finally pulled away. "I suppose you'll be wanting your keys. This one is for the shop, and this one is for your flat. I hope you like our little town."

Bob thrust the two keys into her fist, one brass

and one silver. He grinned up at her for what felt like a lifetime before finally letting go and turning to walk away. He only managed two steps before spinning on his heels, his finger in the air.

"Is this all of your stuff?" Bob asked as he cast an eye at the small pile of boxes, one of which was almost taller than him. "You certainly travel light."

"I wanted a real fresh start." She exhaled and looked over the things she had selected to bring with her on her new adventure. "I have all new furniture arriving soon

"Flat pack?"

"Unfortunately."

"Then I don't envy how you're going to spend your evening!" Bob winked and leaned in. "I have a rather mighty power drill if you'd like to borrow it? Might make the job easier."

"That would be great," Liz said, her mind wandering to the cheap, rather pathetic screwdrivers buried in one of the boxes. "Only if you don't mind?"

"Not at all!" he exclaimed before letting out a jovial chuckle. "You'll find folk are more than helpful 'round here. Here's my card. If you need *anything* just give me a call. Day or night, I don't mind!"

Liz accepted the card as she nodded her thanks. The old man teetered down the street and out of sight. She looked down at the plain white card, which simply read '*Bob Slinger – Landlord,*' above his phone number. She was not certain, but it looked like it had been created using an old, inky typewriter.

"What a peculiar man," she muttered to herself as she unlocked the shop door. "Quite strange indeed."

Her shoes clicked against the dusty hardwood flooring as she walked into the empty store. She crossed her arms and looked around the small space, a smile spreading across her face. It would take a lot of work, but she could not wait until she opened it as her very own arts and crafts store.

Art had been a passion of hers for as long as she could remember. Even though she had not picked up a paintbrush during most of her fifteen years in the police force, she had not been able to put one down in the past two years.

She had settled on Scarlet Cove to start her new

life after seeing a picture of the beautiful English South Coast seaside town on the front of a book in a charity shop. Just from her landlord's hug, she knew small town life would be very different to the one she had left behind in the city. She locked the shop door, wondering how long it would take to adjust to the change.

An hour later, she carried one of the last boxes to the flat above the shop, placing it carefully in the middle of the empty sitting room. She looked around her flat, her heart fluttering with excitement. It was simple, with cream walls and basic fittings, and it lacked the glitz of her city apartment, but it already felt like home. Somehow, it felt like it was where she had always meant to end up, even if she had not expected it to happen when she was forty-two.

Liz turned on her heels to run back downstairs, stopping when she remembered what was inside the box she had just brought up. Bending down, she ripped back the brown tape and carefully plucked out the red leather diary. She stroked the spine, knowing every word contained within its handwritten pages by heart. She flicked to the first page.

'For Liz. So you don't forget any more important dates. Love, Lewis.'

She chuckled sadly, her mind casting back to her thirty-seventh birthday. She had found it strange to receive a diary as a gift, however, the first time she had opened it, she had realised it had already been filled. She flicked through, remembering exactly what lay between its pages. The twenty-second of October had been marked as the anniversary of her first date with Lewis. Every holiday, special occasion, party, and memory had been marked down.

Pulling herself back to the present time, she closed the book and held it tightly to her chest. It had been two years since she had lost her husband, but it was still difficult to fight back the tears. She allowed one to slip down her cheek before she pulled herself together. Lewis had made her promise she would move on with her life and find happiness again.

She placed the book back in the box and turned back to the front door. She did not need a book full of dates to remember Lewis; he was always with her, even in Scarlet Cove.

Leaving the memories behind, she walked into the bright Saturday afternoon, breathing in the fresh seaside air as she pushed the keys into her pocket. The scent of salt and vinegar from the fish and chip shop down the road was thick in the air. Her stomach grumbled, but she could not think about food yet. Seagulls squawked overhead, sounding as hungry as she felt.

Liz picked up the final box, her back creaking. She paused and took in a deep breath. It had been a long day, but she could not believe how glad she was to finally be away from her life in Manchester. With her mind firmly on her future, she turned with the heavy box, hitting a short woman in the process. The collision sent the woman and the box tumbling to the ground. The contents of Liz's bathroom exploded through the cardboard and scattered across the pavement.

"I'm *so* sorry!" Liz apologised as she helped the woman to her feet. "I wasn't watching where I was going."

"That's ok," the woman said as she swept dirt and gravel from her sixties-style dress. "I'm usually the one not looking where I'm going. They say I was born with two left feet." The woman chuckled, before making Liz jump with a snap of her fingers. "You must be our new resident! I'm Nancy Turtle."

"Turtle?" Liz asked, arching a brow as she shook Nancy's hand. "*Unusual* name."

"We're an old family," Nancy exclaimed proudly, her red-tinted lips beaming from ear to ear. "There's been a Turtle in Scarlet Cove for as long as anyone can remember."

"I'm Elizabeth," she replied. "Elizabeth Jones. Not as exciting, but everyone calls me Liz."

Nancy heartily shook Liz's hand again. She would have guessed the woman with the funny name was in her early thirties. She had impossibly thick brown hair with a full fringe that seemed a little too short for her pretty, round face. Thick glasses framed her hazel eyes, magnifying them to double their original size. She was short and curvy, which made Liz feel like a lanky basketball player in comparison.

"We're all very excited about a new shop opening in Scarlet Cove! It's not very often we get new things here." Nancy adjusted her glasses before leaning in. "What's to become of the old sweet shop?

I tried to ask Bob, but he kept it all very hush hush."

"I'm opening an arts and crafts shop," Liz said, unsure of what sort of reaction her admission was going to provoke. "I thought a pretty seaside fishing town like this would have more than a few creative people."

"I *love* art!" Nancy cried, clapping her hands together. "But between you and me, I'm not very good at it. I work at the gallery though, so I get to surround myself with paintings every day. I couldn't ask for a better job."

"I really am sorry," Liz said again, eager to get on with her work. "I'll watch where I'm going next time."

Nancy waved a dismissive hand and said, "It's fine! Gives me a break from being bossed around at the gallery. I work for *the dragon lady*, but if anyone asks, I'll deny saying that. Let me help you gather your things. I'm half responsible, after all."

Before Liz could refuse, Nancy bobbed down and started to gather up the contents of her bathroom cabinet. She peered over her glasses at a couple of the bottles, and even though they were the cheapest Liz had found at a skincare shop, Nancy did not seem to judge, despite her soft and radiant complexion showing that Nancy cared a little more about that stuff than Liz did.

"Let me give you a tour of Scarlet Cove tomorrow," Nancy offered as she picked up a bottle of painkillers and dropped it into the box. "It's the least I can do. You won't know your way around yet, and everyone is dying to meet you."

Liz tried to think of a way to refuse without hurting the feelings of the nice woman who loved art but could not paint. She thought back to her anonymous life in the city, reminded once again how different Scarlet Cove was. If she had bumped into someone back in Manchester, they would not have been so quick to help gather her things.

"I think I'll be okay," Liz said as she picked up the full box. "I'm used to –"

"How about lunchtime?" Nancy jumped in with a smile as she adjusted her glasses. "I'm not working tomorrow."

Liz forced herself to nod. She had not expected to make friends in her first hour in town, but from the pleased look on Nancy's face, Liz knew she had picked a good person to bump into.

"You've been lucky to arrive on market day," Nancy said, appearing eager to continue the conversation. "See the guy with brown hair? That's my boyfriend, Jack, and that's Simon standing next to him." Liz followed Nancy's finger to the paved market square, which was filled with white-roofed stalls. "Jack helps Simon out with his food stall when he can."

"I should really get on with unpacking," Liz said with an awkward smile as she looked down at her box. "Lots to do."

"Me too. Well, not with the unpacking, but – you know what I mean. Busy, *busy*! You should try Simon's ice cream. It's the pride of Scarlet Cove."

Just like her landlord, Nancy hugged Liz, wrapping her arms awkwardly around the large box. Liz stared into the distance and wondered if every person she would come into contact with was going to be so tactile.

With a promise to see Liz tomorrow, Nancy scurried off through the market, no doubt heading back towards the gallery, the location of which Liz would discover tomorrow. Learning of the gallery's existence soothed Liz. It was nice to know she had moved somewhere that appreciated art, and it would not hurt her shop having fellow artists in the small fishing town.

After taking the final box up to her flat, she headed back to the street and locked the door. She had not intended doing anything other than unpacking and starting on a bottle of wine, but the mention of ice cream had piqued her interest. She crossed the road and headed straight for the stall Nancy had pointed out. The men, one with brown hair, and one with dirty blond, greeted her with warm smiles. She was glad when neither of them tried to hug her.

"You must be the newbie," Simon said with an intrigued smile, his bulky muscular frame being the first to not make Liz feel freakishly tall since arriving. "Welcome to Scarlet Cove!"

"How does everyone know about me already?" Liz replied with a curious laugh. "I thought I was slipping in quietly."

"It's a small town," Simon said. "Word travels fast 'round here. We haven't had anyone new arrive in a while, so you've been quite the conversation piece since ol' Bob Slinger spilled the beans about someone finally agreeing to rent his shop and flat."

"I have?"

"You'll love it here," Jack, Nancy's boyfriend, said. "Best place on Earth. What can we do for you?"

Liz looked down at the small stall. It was modest but had a large variety of different flavoured ice creams to choose from, along with more types of cheese than Liz knew existed.

"I'm not the biggest ice cream eater," Liz said as she tapped her hand on her chin. "I'm not sure I'm in the mood for eating a block of cheese though."

The two men chuckled, and even though she thought they were laughing at her at first, she realised there was no judgement in their voices.

"People 'round here love the vanilla," Simon offered. "It's my favourite too."

"You've sold me," Liz said with a nod. "Vanilla it is."

Liz stepped back as Simon scooped a generous amount of the ice cream into a cone.

"First one is on the house," Simon said as he handed Liz the ice cream. "Just don't expect special treatment every time. Word might get 'round that I'm giving away freebies."

Liz accepted the ice cream and smiled her thanks at the kind man. She took his appearance in properly. He had big brown eyes, tousled dirty blond hair, which was coupled with a light dusting of stubble across his cheeks and jaw. He had a soft smile, bright white teeth, and dimples on either side of his dark red lips. Liz could not deny the ice cream seller was handsome, even if he was a similar age to Nancy.

Liz licked the ice cream, the rich and creamy flavour catching her by surprise. Simon leaned back and crossed his arms, appearing more than a little pleased with his handiwork.

"This is really good," Liz said. "Really, *really* good."

"Did you expect any less?" he asked, his brows tensing a little. "I make everything myself up on the family farm. From cow to cone, it's all me."

"That's impressive," Liz said after taking another lick. "You might have changed my mind about ice cream."

"Here," Simon said, reaching into his front jeans pocket to pull out a white napkin. "You've got some —"

Simon wiped Liz's chin where she must have dribbled the melting ice cream. A fleeting moment of eye contact caused an unexpected reaction in Liz's stomach. She did not need a mirror to know she was blushing.

"Thanks," she mumbled. "I'd better make my way back. Lots to do."

With her ice cream in hand, she rushed back to her flat before they could say anything more. She could not quite place her finger on why she felt so embarrassed, but she did. When she reached her flat, she turned back and looked at the stall. Jack nudged Simon, both men grinning like Cheshire cats. Simon met her eyes and gave her a little wave, but she quickly turned to her door, feeling unable to return it. After fumbling with her keys, she unlocked the door and slipped inside. Back in the safety of her flat, she looked down at the ice cream with a smile.

"Too young for you," she whispered to herself as she set off up the stairs to wait for the arrival of her flat pack furniture.

Two

Liz woke the next morning in her new bed, in her new bedroom, with her new bedding. Despite the creak in her lower back that had not been there the previous night, she felt like a brand new woman.

She cast an eye over to the box of clothes she had yet to unpack. Her black detective's hat from the Greater Manchester Police force poked out from the mass of the clothes. It was the only reminder she had brought with her from her old job. She wanted to forget she had ever worn the hat during the job that had taken Lewis away from her, and yet she could not bring herself to part with it.

Her phone vibrated on her bedside table, ripping her from her memory. She smiled when she saw Miles' name flashing on the screen.

"You promised you would call yesterday," he said playfully as soon as she accepted the call. "I thought the local cult might have got to you already."

"I've been busy," she replied, rubbing the sleep from her eyes. "I'm sorry."

"So, how is it?" he asked, slurping what Liz presumed was his morning coffee. "Is it as dull as I predicted? Replaced me already?"

"Of course I have," she mumbled as she dragged herself out of bed. "I almost forgot who you were when I saw your name flashing on the screen. Miles *who*?"

"Very funny," he snapped back. "I just wanted to hear your voice. Is it totally pathetic that I miss you already?"

"Yes," she replied bluntly. "Now if you don't mind, I have a new life to be getting on with."

With a promise to call back when she had something interesting to talk about, she hung up, comforted by the familiar voice.

After having wandered to the small shop on the corner of the street that sold everything she needed to make tea and toast, she quickly prepared her breakfast and sat on her new sofa, which was still wrapped in plastic. She ate her slightly burnt toast and sipped her milky tea, staring at the blank cream wall. She mentally flicked through her collection of paintings, trying to figure out which of her pieces would look best above the small fireplace. She decided she was going to paint something brand new to symbolise her fresh start. After all, Liz in Manchester had been a coffee drinker, but Liz in Scarlet Cove had inexplicably bought tea.

She spent the rest of the morning anticipating Nancy Turtle's arrival. She did not doubt her new acquaintance would turn up exactly at noon to give her the guided tour she had insisted Liz take. Even though she had been resistant to it at first, she had come to realise it would be nice to know where everything was, especially considering she had picked the place based on a picture she had fallen in love with. Just like a beautiful portrait she could paint of a not so attractive person, she knew a picture could be very deceiving.

***

"SO, WHAT DO YOU THINK?" NANCY asked as they left Driftwood Café after filling up on locally made Cornish pasties. "Not bad for a little café, huh?"

"It was delicious," Liz said as she fiddled with her watch. "I really do have a lot to do. I didn't realise how long it would take to unpack. I thought I'd travelled light."

"There's so much *more* to see," Nancy insisted, looping her arm through Liz's "I won't take no for an answer. You'll end up like ol' Mary, who hasn't left her house for three decades if you don't get out and about now."

"An hour," Liz said, unsure of what to do with the arm Nancy was clinging to. "But that's all."

Nancy squealed like a little girl before setting

off, practically dragging Liz along. They walked through town with Nancy pointing out the shops and buildings, giving Liz brief descriptions of everything. She knew so much about everyone and everything, it was obvious she had been born and bred in Scarlet Cove.

"That's the Fish and Anchor, the best pub in Scarlet Cove," Nancy said, pointing but not stopping to let Liz soak it in. "There are a couple of others, but that's the one all the locals go to. The landlady, Shirley Williams, is firm, but lovely. She's been working there since I was born, I think. Ingrained into the fabric of the place. She has a part-time barmaid, Mandy. Not many people think they're too good for Scarlet Cove, but Mandy does. You might want to avoid being served by her."

As the tour continued, they made their way down to the seafront, and to the reason Liz had fallen in love with Scarlet Cove. It was another beautiful day, and the soft whistling of the waves relaxed her in seconds. A slight breeze brought in the scent of fish, something she had never experienced in Manchester unless she had been standing next to the fish stall at one of the markets. Liz leaned against the sea wall and looked out over the water's surface. It stretched out for as far as the eye could see, shining brilliantly under the sun. Fishing boats bobbed up and down, looking like they would fall off the edge of the world if they drifted too far towards the horizon. She looked along the jagged coast, her eyes landing on a tall, white lighthouse. It sat atop a lump of rock, which looked like it was seconds away from crumbling under the pressure of the thrashing waves.

"My dad works there," Nancy said when she caught Liz's gaze. "Tim Turtle. He's been the maintenance guy there –"

"Since you were born?"

"How did you know?" Nancy exclaimed with a grin. "Are you psychic?"

"Lucky guess."

Liz turned and stared up at the town, which had been built on a steep slope. The buildings of all colours looked like they might topple over if the wind hit them right. She shielded her eyes and stared at a castle, which appeared to be the highest point in town.

"That's Scarlet Cove Castle," Nancy said.

"There's been spooky stories surrounding it for as long as I can remember. People say that this place was called something completely different centuries ago, but because of the things that happened up there, they changed the name to Scarlet Cove."

"Why Scarlet Cove?"

"They say the walls were always covered in so much blood that it dripped into the sea." Nancy looked like she was enjoying telling Liz this story. "Creepy, right? People say the medieval ghosts still haunt the grounds. I'm sure I saw a headless woman up there, but Jack thinks I was just drunk."

"Were you drunk?"

"I'd had a drink," Nancy admitted. "But the woman *definitely* didn't have a head. You don't want to go up there at night, that's all I'm saying."

Liz could barely control her laughter, but from the serious expression on Nancy's face, she knew she had to. She had always thought stories of the supernatural were a little far-fetched, and usually the result of decades of local paranoia. If her years in the police force had taught her anything, it was that most things could be explained with a little detective work and some logic.

They continued to walk along the seafront, Nancy pointing out the variety of different shops and B&Bs, but Liz was not taking them in. Her eyes were firmly planted on the calming waves. When they reached the harbour, Liz focussed once again. She recognised it from the picture on the front of the book, but it looked a lot smaller in real life. Old and tired looking boats bobbed up and down, tied to poles sticking out at regular intervals across a wooden walkway. They headed down the walkway to a small office at the end. A man in a sharp suit was standing in front of the office door, his hands planted on his hips as he stared out to sea. He was of average height, and not one of his strikingly icy blond slicked back hairs was out of place. He had a golden tan, and his suit looked expertly tailored to the contours of his body. Everything about the man's appearance told Liz he was probably wealthy.

Nancy cleared her throat, prompting the man to face them. He flashed a dazzling smile, and even though his teeth were perfectly straight and porcelain white, he seemed to have too many for his mouth. Liz had never thought she had a type, but she knew this man was not it, despite being classically handsome.

"Nancy, what a lovely surprise," he said, his perfect diction sticking out amongst the more casual accents Liz had heard. "What brings you here?"

"Christopher, this is Liz," Nancy said, pushing Liz forward. "She's new in town."

Feeling like a prize pig at the meat market, Liz stood awkwardly in front of Christopher and smiled. He took her hand and kissed it, his crystal blue eyes not wavering from hers.

"Liz must be short for Elizabeth," he said softly. "A very beautiful, classic name, I must say. It is a pleasure to put a face to the mysterious new resident I've been hearing so much about. Do you like fish?"

"I suppose," Liz said, discreetly wiping her hand on the back of her jeans. "I haven't really given it much thought. I'm not much of a cook."

"Chris delivers to The Sea Platter," Nancy said. "Best restaurant in town."

"It's *Christopher*," he corrected her with a strained smile. "And yes, I deliver my fish there. I run this harbour, you see, and The Sea Platter is one of the many restaurants I deliver to. You must visit sometime."

Liz did not know what to say, so she smiled and nodded. Something about the way the man spoke put her on edge. It reminded her of the way guilty people would talk in interviews when they thought they could lie their way through questioning. Reminding herself she had left that life behind, she tried to force herself to relax. She smiled a little easier at the harbour owner, but an incoming boat caught his attention, ending their brief conversation.

"Would you excuse me," he said, resting a hand on Liz's shoulder. "I have business to attend to. It was very nice meeting you, Elizabeth. I hope we get a chance to talk again." He kissed her hand again before turning to Nancy. "Bye," he added, almost as an afterthought.

Compared to the other townsfolk she had met so far, Christopher stuck out in every way.

"Is everyone so touchy feely in this place?" Liz asked as she wiped her hand on her jeans again.

"You're so funny," Nancy laughed, slapping Liz on the arm, the action alone confirming her question.

They were about to leave, but raised voices from the recently arrived boat caught their attention.

They turned on their heels and looked in the direction of the commotion.

"I don't *care* how long you've been here, you are *useless*!" a bearded man shouted at a boy who did not look any older than twenty. "You *aren't* cut out for this job, and you *don't* show any signs of improving, Adam!"

"Frank, I'm *trying*!" the lanky teenager pleaded. "You *know* I'm trying! I *need* this job."

"That's not good enough! You're lazy. You don't care about this job one bit. Don't think I don't know what you've been up to!" Frank shouted again. "I'm sorry, but you're fired!"

"This is because of Mandy, isn't it?" Adam cried back. "This *isn't* fair!"

Frank clenched his fists by his side, and for a moment, Liz readied herself out of habit to jump in. To her surprise, the bearded man stormed down the walkway and along the seafront. A small brown and white beagle jumped over the edge of the boat and ran after him, its tongue lolling out of the side of its mouth.

"Who was that?" Liz asked as she watched Frank disappear.

"Frank is Chris' head fisher," Nancy whispered as they watched Adam talk to Christopher. "Not the nicest of men. Remember the barmaid I told you to stay away from? That's her father."

"Mandy?" Liz thought aloud. "Adam said '*this is because of Mandy*'."

"I always thought Frank liked Adam," Nancy said. "Frank's not the easiest guy to work with. He is set in his ways, but Adam seemed like the right sort of kid to listen. Frank will probably see sense tomorrow. I bet they're crying over spilt milk. You know what men are like."

"Or spilt fish guts."

"You're so *funny*, Liz!" Nancy exclaimed again, slapping her on the arm once more. "You're going to fit right in!"

They left the harbour and set off back to Liz's flat. When they were outside, Nancy gave her another hug, and Liz was finding that she was not seizing up as much now that she was getting used to it.

"I hope you enjoyed your tour," Nancy said with a fiddle of her glasses. "It's nice to make a new friend."

"It is," Liz said. "I'll see you around."

Liz waved Nancy off, more than sure that she would see her on a regular basis. She did not mind. After spending the afternoon with her, she had grown to enjoy her quirks.

She pulled her keys out of her bag but turned when she heard something trundling along the street towards her. She spotted a tractor slowly making its way up the steep road. When she noticed Simon was the driver, a little smile took her lips by surprise.

"How's this old place treating you?" Simon shouted down at her as he slowed the noisy tractor to a shuddering halt, the scent of diesel thick in the air. "I hope you're settling in."

"I think I'm getting the hang of it," she called up at him, shielding her eyes from the sun. "Big tractor."

Liz looked around Simon and spotted a little girl in the passenger seat. She had blonde pigtails, denim dungarees, and big glasses. She hummed a tune Liz did not recognise as she kicked her heels against the seat, her feet barely scraping the floor.

"This is Ellie," Simon said when he noticed Liz staring. "My little sister. Say hello, Ellie."

Ellie hid behind Simon's shoulder and peeked at Liz through the strands of hair that had fallen out of her pigtails. She gave Liz a shy smile, her two front teeth bigger than the rest, but she did not speak.

"Hi, Ellie," Liz said, her years of working with children at the station softening her voice. "I'm Liz. How old are you?"

Ellie bobbed her head around her brother's shoulder again, her shyness seeming to quickly disappear. She edged forward along the seat and twirled one of her pigtails around her finger.

"I'm seven," she announced, holding up seven fingers. "Seven and a quarter."

"Aren't you a big girl?" Liz said with pretend shock. "I remember when I was seven, but that was a long time ago now."

A grin spread from ear to ear on Ellie's face, her two front teeth sticking out over her bottom lip

"Are you Simon's girlfriend?" Ellie asked as she wiped her runny nose with the back of her hand. "He said the new woman was pretty yesterday."

"*Ellie!*" Simon cried, his cheeks blushing. "Why don't you finish your lollipop?"

Ellie pulled an unwrapped lollipop from her

pocket and crammed it in her mouth as she resumed kicking her feet against the chair.

"She doesn't know what she's saying," Simon stuttered. "You know what kids are like."

"Heading anywhere nice in this thing?" Liz asked as she slapped the side of the tractor, choosing to ignore what Ellie had said.

"We're delivering some cheese to the café," he said as he reached in the back to retrieve a wrapped block. "It's as fresh as it comes. Ellie insisted we take the tractor. She loves the thing, don't you, Ellie?"

"Is my tongue a funny colour?" Ellie asked as she stared down her nose, ignoring her brother.

"It's very – *blue,*" Liz assured her. "Been eating Smurfs?"

Ellie chuckled as she continued to lick her lollipop. Liz smiled, not wanting the sadness to take over her. Lewis had always said they would have kids when their careers quietened down, but she had long since come to accept that would never happen now.

"Here you go." Simon passed Liz the wrapped cheese, breaking her thought. "It may not look like much, but looks can sometimes be deceiving."

"Thank you," Liz said as she looked down at the

block in her hands. "Everyone in this town is so welcoming. I'm not used to it."

"We try," he said, blushing again. "I hope we're much nicer than city folk. Must be off. We still have deliveries to do, so I'll see you around. Enjoy the cheese."

She waved them off as Simon turned the tractor and headed down the road. Ellie spun around in her chair and waved enthusiastically at Liz as she stuck out her bright blue tongue. When the tractor disappeared, Liz stared down at the cheese, wondering how it could be any different from the stuff she normally bought at the supermarket.

When she returned to her flat, she spent a couple of hours unpacking before setting up her easel. The rest of the unboxing could wait until she had something beautiful to hang above her fireplace.

She knew once the shop opened up below, she would have less time to paint, so she was going to enjoy it while she could. She had painted almost everyday since Lewis' death. Thinking about the past sent a shiver down her spine, but she forced herself to think of something else. She had spent enough time grieving, and it had not done her any favours.

She dragged her easel over to the small window overlooking the street and placed a small canvas on the ridge. While she mulled over what she wanted to paint, she flicked the kettle on and looked over the different boxes of tea she had bought from the shop that morning, settling on cranberry and cinnamon. After placing the tea bag and newly hot water into a mug, she walked over to her easel.

She looked out of the window as the day started to fade, the peachy sunset astounding her. The pinks, oranges, and purples engulfed the sky, inspiring her in an instant. Liz sipped on her tea as she fingered through her box of oil paints. When she decided what she was going to do, she balanced her paintbrushes on the windowsill and got to work.

She looked out at the fishing town, sketching as she went. She traced a few buildings here and there, and then drew the castle on the hill. When she was happy with the outline, she started to paint. She settled on using the same colours she could see out of the window

As her brush hit the canvas, her brain switched off, entering her happy place. Her fingers danced across her easel, completely submerged in her work as though she was the conduit and someone else was the painter.

The hours passed by in an instant, as did the sunset. She worked from memory, the beautiful burning colours etched in her mind's eye. She took a final sip of her tea, not minding that it had gone cold. When she looked at the clock, she let out a yawn, not wanting to believe it was already past midnight. She finally set down her brush; the details would have to be added another time.

The painting had drained her, so she quickly prepared a bowl of cereal. She had never been much of a cook, but she had not needed to be with Lewis. Her meals now consisted of things she could pour into a bowl and whatever would fit in the microwave.

After wolfing down the bland cereal, she washed the bowl, and as she was drying her hands, she looked at the unopened cheese on her kitchen counter. She unwrapped it, picked a crumb from the corner, and popped it into her mouth. Just like the ice cream, she was surprised by how delicious it was. Picking off another chunk, she tossed it into her mouth as she walked to her bedroom.

After climbing into bed, her mind wandered back to the argument she had witnessed at the harbour, but before she could focus on the details, she drifted off into a deep sleep.

Three

L iz took herself and her easel down to the harbour the next morning. She left her sunset painting in the flat, deciding she wanted to make use of the stunning sea views Scarlet Cove had to offer. They were, after all, the reason she had picked the place for her fresh start.

She set up away from the boats and Christopher's office, in front of a bar called

Coastline Cabaret, which was next to a small souvenir shop called Tidal Trinkets. People passed by, smiling at her curiously, but nobody interrupted her, which was just how she liked things.

As she stared out to sea, she thought of the times she had gone out and painted in nature. During her days in college, she had loved to paint countryside landscapes, but since rediscovering her love of painting, her art had revolved around dull cityscapes and urban scenes. The multitude of blue shades in the sky and sea excited her. She unclipped her box of oil paints and looked at some of the barely touched shades she was determined to use today.

She pulled out her binoculars and stared out at the small boats on the horizon. After sampling Simon's cheese again that morning, she was excited to see what other food Scarlet Cove had to offer. She had not even considered that she was probably going to be eating a lot more seafood until meeting Christopher the previous day.

As she quickly sketched out the scene in front of her, she thought about how unprepared she had been for the move. In a way, she had wanted to know as little as possible about the place she was moving to so she could experience it first-hand. Resting her pencil against the canvas, she closed her eyes and inhaled the salty sea air, the only sound coming from the seagulls above. It was pure bliss.

That bliss was quickly interrupted when a distant barking dog caused her to run her pencil against a crudely sketched fishing boat. She flipped the pencil over and rubbed out the line before checking that she had not damaged the canvas. When she was satisfied that it was fine, she started to mix the perfect base shade for the sky.

"You're a painter?" a voice called from behind. "How fascinating."

She turned to see Christopher walking towards her, hands deep in his trouser pockets. He was wearing another well-fitted business suit, which Liz could tell was expensive.

"I don't have a creative bone in my body," he said when she did not reply. "I was always more interested in numbers."

"It's a good release," Liz said as she washed her custom shade over the upper portion of the canvas. "It's free therapy."

Christopher stood back and watched her paint

for a moment. She could feel her hand moving a little less freely than usual, and she was starting to second-guess her strokes. She lifted the brush off the canvas and began to slowly mix another shade of blue in the hope Christopher would leave her in peace.

"All of those boats are mine," he said, wafting his finger in the direction of the half a dozen boats in the distance. "I've built myself a sturdy fishing empire here. I'm thinking of expanding out across the coast when the time is right."

"Sounds like a good idea," she mumbled noncommittally as she eased a little white paint out of the tube and onto the palette. "I suppose you have a lot of work to do."

"Not until the boats come back," he said, leaning against the wall and facing away from the view. "How are you settling in?"

"Quite alright," she replied, wincing as the distant dog began to bark again. "Although I envisioned this being a more *peaceful* activity."

"I've never understood the point of art myself," Christopher mumbled, appearing a little distant. "My sister is mad for the stuff."

Liz scratched at her red wavy hair with the end of the paintbrush. She looked at the glistening wash of blue on her canvas and realised she was not going to spend the morning painting by the sea like she had hoped. She considered taking a picture of the view and retreating back to the safety of her flat, but it would not be the same. She had moved to Scarlet Cove to paint by the sea, and she was determined to do just that.

The second her paintbrush touched the canvas again, she jumped and painted over a blank space she had been saving for the sun when the dog barked again.

"Where *is* that coming from?" Liz asked, the frustration loud in her voice.

"Sounds like Paddy, Frank's beagle. They should be back by now, but I suppose it's taking longer since he sacked Adam."

Liz picked up her binoculars again and scanned the boats. She landed on the one she recognised Frank steering back into the harbour yesterday. She spotted the beagle, barking wildly at the air, but she did not spot Frank. She watched for a moment and waited for him to bob up from below deck, but nothing happened.

"I can't see him," Liz said, the binoculars crammed against her eyes. "Maybe he's hurt?"

"He's probably drunk." Christopher snatched the binoculars from Liz and stared out at sea. "Everything's tiny!"

Liz pulled the binoculars from his grip and turned them around.

"He's become so unreliable," he continued after an awkward chuckle. "Has a hip flask with him wherever he goes now. He's a shadow of the man he was when I first bought the company."

Liz stood up and shielded her eyes from the sun. She could just make out Paddy jumping up onto a box and looking overboard. He barked furiously at the water, looking as though he might jump in, but he stopped himself.

"If he's passed out on deck, it wouldn't be the first time," Christopher said as he tossed the binoculars back to Liz. "I can't keep letting him get away with this. Why do you have binoculars anyway? Are you a painter or a spy?"

"They're good for seeing details," she said quickly, not wanting to admit they were the ones from her detective days. "What if something has happened? Paddy sounds distressed."

"It's the boat I'm worried about," Christopher replied. "If Frank is drunk out there and he hasn't dropped the anchor, the thing could drift off into the unknown."

"And what about Frank?"

"They're expensive boats," he snapped. "Frank is replaceable. I need to go out there and bring it back in, and I might fire the fella while I'm at it! There are only so many times I can let him get away with these things!"

Christopher checked his chunky gold watch, which looked like it cost more than a year's worth of rent for Liz's flat. He ran his hands through his slicked back hair and let out a tired sigh as though the whole ordeal was nothing more than a minor inconvenience.

"How are you getting out there?" Liz asked as she peered over her canvas at the stranded boat.

"I have a speedboat on hand."

"Can I come?" Liz replied. "It would be nice to see Scarlet Cove from the sea."

Christopher looked sceptically at Liz for a

moment, but he smiled and nodded to let her know it was okay. She quickly packed up her painting things and carried them down the seafront to the harbour. She left her easel and paints in his office before climbing into his boat.

"Hold on tight," he said as he started up the engine. "The water can be too choppy for some women."

"I'm *sure* I'll manage," Liz said, not telling him it was not her first time in a boat.

Christopher set off, steering the small boat expertly, proving that he had done it many times before. They bounced up and down on the water, the wind licking Liz's face, her wavy hair catching the salt spray. The way Christopher looked back at her with a smug grin proved how little he was concerned about his head fisher being drunk and passed out on the deck.

As they got closer to the fishing boat, the speedboat let out an ear-splitting groan and halted, thick puffs of grey smoke billowing from the engine.

"What's happening?"

"I don't know," Christopher replied smacking the engine with a forceful fist. "This has never happened before."

Christopher ran his hands through his dishevelled hair as he looked desperately back to the shore.

Paddy's barks grew louder and more aggravated, unsettling Liz. She had owned a beagle growing up, and it had been her best friend. Losing him had been so painful, she had never dared put herself through the heartache again. She had considered getting a pet as part of her new start, but she was sure she was more suited to a goldfish than anything else, and even that seemed like more responsibility than she could handle.

"Can't you *do* something?" Liz cried, growing more and more worried. "Maybe it's run out of fuel?"

From where they were, she could see the boat, but she still could not see Frank, only Paddy.

"*Frank?*" Christopher shouted now standing, undeniably irritated. "If you can hear me, *you're fired!*"

Liz opened her mouth to speak but immediately stopped when she saw something orange floating in the water. When she realised it was a lifejacket, and it was attached to a man, she let out a small gasp, her heart fluttering in her chest. She pulled Christopher back down to her level, her hands shaking.

"*Christopher*," Liz mumbled, Paddy's barks drowning her out. "I think that's Frank."

Christopher leaned over the side of the boat as Liz reached out and grabbed the orange lifejacket as it drifted by. With all of her strength, she turned the body around, her stomach knotting when she looked in the glassy eyes staring up at her through a mess of fish netting wrapped around his face. No matter how many bodies she had seen in her lifetime, it never got any easier.

"He's dead," Liz said after gulping hard. "Frank is dead."

Four

L iz accepted an invitation from Nancy to go to the pub the next day, despite not getting a decent night's sleep. She had hesitated at first but decided it would be a good idea to get to know more of the townsfolk, especially since she had just fished a dead one out of the water.

When Liz arrived at the Fish and Anchor, Nancy was already waiting outside for her.

"Here she is," Nancy said as she pulled Liz into a hug. "Our new local *celebrity*. Everyone is talking about you finding Frank's body. Jack and Simon are already here. They're dying to find out what happened – *although*, I don't think '*dying*' is the right word."

Nancy chuckled to herself as she pulled on the door. The Fish and Anchor was not a trendy cocktail bar like the places Liz was used to, but it was exactly what she had expected from a fishing pub. It was cramped and dark, and smelt of stale ale and fire smoke. Every inch of the walls was covered in local fishing memorabilia, and it was packed out despite the early hour. The mismatched chairs complemented the oak tables, and instead of the usual carpet, the floor was made of wood. The bar stretched across the right side of the room, with almost a dozen fishermen propped up at it with pints in their hands, none of them talking to each other. It was packed with the spirit and character brewery-owned chain pubs tried to replicate, but she could feel the authenticity in every particle of the building. Somehow, Liz already felt right at home.

She followed Nancy into the corner of the room,

where Jack and Simon were sitting under a large anchor, which jutted out of the wall at such an unsecure angle, she was sure it was breaking more than a few health and safety laws. Both men smiled at her, but Liz noticed that Simon's seemed a little wider.

"*Hey*," Jack and Simon said in unison as the two women sat down.

Liz took the seat next to Simon, and Nancy sat next to her boyfriend. They immediately started talking in hushed voices, giggling like school children. Simon glanced at Liz and rolled his eyes playfully.

"Young love, huh?" Simon said, so close that Liz could smell his musky aftershave. "You wouldn't think they've only been together for a year."

"Looks like the honeymoon period to me," Liz said, smiling at the loved-up couple. "They should enjoy it while they can."

"We *are* here, ya'know." Simon tossed a scrunched up napkin their way.

"Sorry!" Nancy exclaimed, her soft cheeks blushing. "I feel like I haven't seen him in years."

"You saw me this morning," Jack said with a

laugh as he kissed her cheek. "But I missed you too."

Liz remembered what it felt like to be that in love. She and Lewis had been completely inseparable at the beginning of their relationship, and it had not changed much after they had wed. She tried to visualise his face, but it was getting harder to remember the finer details.

"I heard what happened to Frank," Jack said, pulling Liz back to the present. "It's all people can talk about. They're saying it was some drunken accident, and that he got wasted on the boat, got caught up in some net, and fell overboard."

"Poor fella," Simon said after sipping his pint, some of the foam on his top lip. "He was always carrying that hip flask with him. He'd even bring it in here, but Shirley never stood for that. He did like his whiskey a little too much."

"Did you know him well?" Liz asked casually, intrigued by the man she had pulled out of the water.

"He'd lived in Scarlet Cove all of his life, like the rest of us," Nancy started, edging forward, seeming excited to be the one to fill Liz in. "His father was a fisherman, and his father before him was too. People always said Frank was gutted when he had a daughter."

"Gutted like a fish?" Jack suggested with a wink.

"*Jack*!" Nancy cried, holding back a smirk. "You're *wicked*! Anyway, it's not like you don't get women fishers, but it's not as common, is it?"

"That's why he was so glad when Adam showed such an interest in the business," Jack took over from Nancy. "Which is why I don't understand why Frank's last action in this town was to fire the kid."

"We've always had fishing in Scarlet Cove, but Fishy Chris really stepped it up," Nancy mumbled as she scanned the food menu. "It used to just be a couple of boats, but Chris is buying new ones all the time. Never seems content with his lot in life."

"Fishy Chris?" Liz asked.

"*Christopher*," Simon mumbled. "Our lord and master, or so he likes to think. He hates that little nickname, but we're all rather fond of it."

Nancy snickered behind the menu as she caught Liz's eyes. Liz could not help but laugh. It almost reminded her of being back in school again.

"Is he here?" Liz asked, turning and looking around the small pub. "I don't see him."

"He wouldn't be caught dead in here unless they started serving champagne on tap with a side order of caviar," Jack said, which was accompanied by another giggle from Nancy. "Although don't say that *too* loud. Most of those fishermen at the bar are on Fishy Chris' payroll."

"He's always thought he was too good for this place," Simon explained, imitating Christopher's more refined accent. "I'm surprised he's stayed in Scarlet Cove for as long as he has. People say he's looking for a wife, but most women know there's not much behind that charm."

"Watch out, Liz," Nancy giggled. "You're *just* his type."

Jack choked on his pint as he caught Liz's eyes. She looked around the table, unsure if that had been a compliment or an insult. Was that why Nancy had thrust her in front of him during their little tour?

"Leave her alone," Simon said. "You don't want to scare her out of town before she's settled in."

"Back to Frank," Nancy said quickly. "His daughter, Mandy, works behind the bar. She's the one with the strawberry blonde hair and too much makeup."

Nancy nodded at the bar, so Liz turned in her chair to stare at the barmaid, who seemed more interested in her nails than serving the customers.

"Her dad has just died, and she's here working?" Liz mumbled, almost to herself. "That's odd."

"They weren't that close," Simon explained. "After her mum died a few years back, Frank and Mandy haven't really seen eye to eye. She only really bothered with him when she needed money."

"Looking that fake takes a lot of upkeep," Nancy mumbled over the top of the menu. "It takes a lot of money to look that –"

"*Apparently*, her mother left a lot of money to Frank when she died," Jack jumped in. "Mandy didn't get a penny, which everyone thought was odd because Mandy was always closer to her mum than Frank, but they were always a strange family."

"You would never have thought ol' Frank was sitting on a pot of gold though," Nancy said. "He dressed like a fisherman and always smelt of fish."

"Funny, that?" Simon replied with a roll of his eyes. "Anyone would think he *was* a fisherman."

"You *know* what I mean," Nancy fired back as she adjusted her glasses. "If I had thousands in the bank, I wouldn't keep working for the dragon lady at the gallery. I'd treat myself."

"Did Frank have anyone to treat?" Liz asked. "Anyone special in his life?"

The trio looked awkwardly at one another, letting Liz know there had been someone special in Frank's life. Nancy and Jack stared over Liz's shoulder and looked into the corner of the room. Liz craned her neck and looked at a pretty pixie-like woman with black hair. She was staring vacantly into a glass of wine, but it looked untouched.

"He was seeing Laura," Jack said, nodding to the woman in the corner. "She's thirty-seven, and Frank was –"

"Almost at retirement age," Simon interjected before sipping his pint. "Gives me the creeps."

"He was fifty-three," Jack corrected him. "A lifetime on the sea was not kind to that man. I feel like I should go over and say something to her, but I don't know what to say."

"Just leave her," Nancy suggested, resting her hand on Jack's. "She looks like she wants space."

Liz looked around the pub, suddenly noticing that most of the people around her were glancing periodically at the grieving woman. Liz knew exactly what that felt like, and she knew Nancy was right; Laura would want to be left alone to process what had just happened.

"So," Liz said, her mind piecing together the information. "He has a daughter that he wasn't particularly close with and a younger girlfriend."

"Laura is still married too," Nancy said as she leaned in. "Her relationship with Frank caused *quite* the scandal."

"They're separated," Jack mentioned. "But people say that Laura was seeing Frank before she was officially separated from Michael. Poor fella was devastated."

"You listen to too much gossip," Simon stated before sipping his pint. "Anyone would think you were an old fishwife, Jacky Boy."

"It's just what I heard," he snapped back, narrowing his eyes on his friend. "It's not like there's much else going on around here. It didn't take her long to move on. I have nothing against her, I just don't really know her because I always thought Laura and Michael were happy. They were childhood sweethearts. They're a couple of years older than us, but it's a small town, so you think you know people, that's all I'm saying."

"Appearances can be deceiving," Liz said. "Why don't we get some drinks in?"

"Good idea," Jack said, springing up in an instant. "Is lager okay for everyone? You *have* to try the Scarlet Cove Brew, Liz. It's world famous."

"Sounds good to me," Liz said.

"I didn't take you for a lager sort of girl," Simon said with an arched brow.

"Well, maybe you've got the wrong impression of me," she said back at him, not remembering the last time anyone called her a '*girl*'. "Although between you and me, you're right, but Jack looked excited about the brew, and I couldn't say no."

Simon chuckled, flashing her his boyish dimples. They stared at each other for a silent moment as Nancy continued to look over the menu. Liz's stomach squirmed, forcing her to look away. She coughed, hoping it would explain why she suddenly red-faced.

"They've added a tandoori section to the menu," Nancy mumbled absently. "How exotic."

Jack returned with a tray containing four frothy

pints of Scarlet Cove Brew. Liz focussed on the full glasses for the sake of something to do. She gratefully accepted her pint, avoiding looking in Simon's direction. She lifted the glass to her lips, Jack staring expectantly at her as he placed the other pints on the table. Liz was pleased when she did not gag.

"Really nice," Liz said after a small sip. "Good recommendation."

Jack beamed at her as he sat back down next to Nancy. They looped fingers as they sipped their pints. The pub busied around them, but silence descended on their table. With her glass to her lips, Liz looked back at Laura again. She wanted to let the poor woman know it would get easier with time, but she knew talk was cheap when it came to grief.

"How long were they together?" Liz asked.

"About three years, I think," Nancy said as she pushed her glasses up her button nose.

"It was more than a fling then?"

"Oh, yeah." Nancy nodded enthusiastically. "They were like two love sick puppies. It made it easier that Michael accepted them and didn't make things awkward."

"He's a top fella," Jack said with a nod. "Most wouldn't be so gracious about another bloke stealing their missus."

"It didn't help that Mandy and Laura used to be friends though," Nancy said. "They definitely didn't have a happy step-mother and daughter relationship."

"They're practically the same age," Simon added. "Mandy seemed to think Laura was only with her father for the money."

"Is that what you all think?" Liz asked.

"People talk," Nancy said with a shrug. "I don't know what to think. Yes, there was an age-gap, but they did seem happy together. Didn't take Laura long to move in with Frank. You never know what happens behind closed doors though. Like you said, Liz, appearances can be deceptive."

"Why do I feel like I'm being interviewed at the station?" Jack asked with a laugh. "Reminds me of that time I got drunk when I was fourteen, and I stole that tractor."

"*My* tractor," Simon added.

"*You* gave me the keys!" Jack cried. "You were *just* as drunk as I was."

The two men shared a knowing look as they laughed, letting Liz know their friendship likely stretched back to birth. She wondered if she was the only person in town who had not been born and raised in Scarlet Cove, which made her immediate acceptance feel all the stranger.

"I was a police officer for fifteen years," Liz said coolly. "I retired with the rank of detective. Old habits die hard, I suppose."

Jack choked on his pint and spat the mouthful back into the glass. His cheeks flushed, a sweat seeming to break out on his forehead.

"You never told me that," Nancy said with an excited smile. "You're getting more interesting by the day, Liz Jones!"

"It feels like it was so long ago already," Liz said. "It almost happened to a different person in a different life."

"I can just imagine you now, running around catching criminals," Nancy said, her fingers forming a gun to scope out the room. "No wonder you were the one to find Frank's body! I bet you sniffed it out from the shore."

"It was mainly a lot of paperwork," she said

sheepishly as she realised she had broken the promise she had made to keep her past quiet so she could have a completely fresh start. "I'm all about the art now."

"Why did you retire?" Simon asked, turning in his seat to face her with a curious smile. "You really are quite surprising."

Liz opened her mouth to speak, unsure of what she was going to say. She was almost glad when a brawl erupted at the bar, giving her an excuse to look away from Simon. They all watched the two fishermen fight in a drunken fluster, and by the time the tough landlady, Shirley, pulled them apart, the interest in her past life had been dropped.

Liz stuck around and finished her pint, chatting idly about her plans for her shop. When she felt it was time to leave, Nancy hugged her tightly, and Jack and Simon both shook her hand. Just like his wider smile when she had arrived, Liz was sure Simon's soft grip on her hand had been longer than strictly necessary.

After leaving the Fish and Anchor, Liz headed to the harbour in search of Christopher. Considering the dreadful experience they had shared only the day before, she wanted to make sure he was okay, despite what her new friends thought about him.

As she passed Coastline Cabaret on the seafront, she noticed Laura, who had slipped out before Liz had finished her pint. She was standing with a tall man, who made her look even more pixie-like. They were arguing in hushed tones, Laura's hands flapping about dramatically, and her eyes bright and puffy.

When they saw her approaching, they drifted into the alley next to the bar and out of earshot. Liz did not make it obvious that she was trying to eavesdrop as she walked past, but she strained her ears, breathing quietly. She did not pick up anything, but she was sure she had heard Frank's name pop up.

When she arrived at the office, she was surprised to see Frank's beagle, Paddy, curled up in front of Christopher's desk. Liz instinctively crouched down and scratched behind his floppy ears. He beamed up at her, his eyes half closed and his mouth forming into something that resembled a smile.

"Hello, Paddy," Liz cooed.

The beagle responded by generously licking her

fingers.

"He seems to like you," Christopher said, barely looking up from the paperwork he was looking over. "He's been running circles around me all day."

"What are you going to do with him now that Frank is gone?" Liz asked, stroking down the dog's soft back. "He's so cute."

"He's going straight to the shelter," Christopher said coolly. "There's nothing else I can do for him. I certainly don't have time to look after a dog."

"What about Frank's daughter?" Liz suggested.

"*Mandy?*" Christopher scoffed. "The only thing that girl would take off her father is his money."

Liz looked down into the dog's eyes and tried to imagine him sitting in a tiny cage, hoping and praying that someone would come and take him home. Her heart broke for him.

"I'll take him," she said. "He's been through enough."

"Are you sure?"

"I think so," she said with a nod. "I'm going to have a lot of time on my hands. He can be my shop dog. Customers will love him."

"I'm sure," Christopher mumbled with

disinterest.

Liz stood up and looked down at her new companion. As though he knew they were about to become roommates, he stood up and settled by her feet.

"I actually came to ask about Frank," Liz said. "I wanted to check if you were okay."

"I'm fine," Christopher said dismissively as he flipped over a piece of paper. "And so is the boat. I'll have another fisher in it by the end of the week. I've already had all these applications."

Liz held her tongue. She was starting to see why her new friends spoke less than favourably about Christopher.

"Any news on how he died?" she asked.

"It was just a drunken accident," Christopher said airily as he looked up at her with his toothy smile. "There is nothing more to it. Was bound to happen sooner or later."

Before Liz could interrogate him further, Christopher handed her Paddy's lead, and told her he was busy. He smiled apologetically before practically shoving her out of the small office. They said their goodbyes before he closed the door and got back to work. She looked down at Paddy and smiled before setting off. She was not the only one who deserved a fresh start.

Liz arrived back at the flat with her new friend. After placing a beef stew for one in the microwave, she looked around her flat, wondering if there were anything she would need to do to make it more dog friendly. She decided she was going to make a list the following day and buy everything she could remember that dogs needed, but for tonight, they would be fine as they were.

As her microwave hummed, she flicked through her box of vinyl records, pausing when she found Lewis' favourite album. She carefully pulled the twelve-inch disk out of the sleeve and turned it over in her fingers before placing it on the player. She dropped the needle into place, and the soft disco melodies of ABBA's *Arrival* album filled the flat.

She sat at the table with the meal for one and scooped some into a dish for Paddy, blowing on it to cool it down. She lit the candle in the middle of the table and unscrewed the lid off a fresh bottle of wine.

She looked down at Paddy with a smile as

Dancing Queen played in the background.

"It's just you and me now, little guy."

Five

L iz stirred from her sleep, something wet grazing against her face. Trying to cling onto the dream that was already slipping away, she rolled over, brushing her wet cheek.

"*Huh?*" she forced her eyes open and stared into her new beagle's eyes. "Oh, it's you."

Paddy bounced up at her and licked her chin, his wagging tail slapping against her exposed leg. She scratched behind his ear as she looked around her bedroom, her body screaming out for caffeine.

"You want to go for a walk?" she mumbled as she rubbed her eyes. "Let's grab a coffee on the way."

Paddy bounced off the bed and ran in a circle, his nails scratching against the floorboards. She was not sure if dogs' grieving processes were anything like humans', but she was glad he did not seem too affected by the loss of his master.

After quickly dressing in faded jeans and a thin blue jumper, she clipped the lead onto Paddy's red collar and set off. He practically dragged her down the stairs to the street. When they were out in the bright daylight, he immediately cocked his leg against the front of her shop and relieved himself. Liz let out a yawn and looked around her new home as she tried to wake up. She had an uneasy feeling that she had dreamed about drowning last night.

After grabbing a large latte with an extra espresso shot from Driftwood Café, she headed for the shore. As she walked along the pier, Paddy eagerly pulling, she was glad she had chosen a jumper. She knew it was probably quite warm away from the coast, but the breeze was less forgiving.

The pier was alive with activity. She walked along it, smiling at the people as she passed them. A couple of people looked down at the dog, but none of them screamed that she had stolen a dead man's companion.

There was a small rundown amusement arcade called Sea Slots at the end of the pier. The sign blinked in the bright sunlight, which Liz was sure made a more impressive impact in the darker hours.

Seeing no evidence of a '*No Dogs Allowed*' sign, she headed inside with Paddy by her feet. The machines flashed brightly in the dimly lit room, a dozen different tunes coming from them. She took in the old place as she walked across the well-worn carpet, the faint scent of old money and popcorn tickling her nostrils. Paddy jumped back when a group of children sprinted past, followed by their less enthusiastic parents. She paused by the air hockey machine and watched as a young couple played a determined match. The girl scored and jumped up and down in celebration.

Liz turned to leave, but she stopped in her tracks when she spotted Adam and Mandy talking in the corner. She almost left them to it, but her curiosity caught the better of her. She was not entirely convinced there was something suspicious surrounding Frank's death, but she could not shake the feeling there was more to be learned. Deciding eavesdropping on the man's former apprentice and daughter was a good place to start, she tiptoed over and hid behind a penny slot machine.

"I *know* he was my father, and I *am* upset over what happened, but he *was* a drunk, and he *fired* you," Mandy said in an agitated tone.

"Do you really think that's how he died? Come on, even *he* isn't that stupid," Adam said.

"How should I know?" Mandy shot back defensively. "Aren't you mad he fired you?"

"Of course I am, but I didn't want the man *dead*! Simon offered me some casual work at the farm, so that's not a problem. Before he - *before* the accident, he had been acting strangely. He constantly looked exhausted."

"Trouble in paradise?" Mandy spat back.

"He never really mentioned anything about Laura when we worked, but he knew about us," Adam said.

"It's a small town and people talk. Secrets are

hard to hide," Mandy said with obvious venom. "At least we can be together in peace now."

"You must know-"

But before Adam could finish his sentence, Paddy barked and yanked on his lead. Adam and Mandy quickly turned around, spotting Liz in an instant. Liz quickly scrabbled with her purse and pulled out some change. She added pennies into the machine, knowing it was a feeble attempt at a recovery. Mandy looked Liz up and down before striding off and flipping her strawberry blonde hair over her shoulders. Adam narrowed his eyes on Liz before scurrying after Mandy.

Liz dropped a penny into the machine, but she was not paying attention. She thought about what Mandy had said before Paddy had interrupted them. 'At least we can be together now'. Her mind flicked back to seeing Frank firing Adam, and she was sure Adam had mentioned Mandy as one of the reasons for being fired. She did not have to be a genius to figure out that Frank and Laura's was not the only age-gap relationship in Scarlet Cove. She turned and watched as the teenager and woman in her late twenties walked out of the arcade.

Paddy barked again as a shelf of brown pennies fell off the edge of the machine and into the tray below.

"My undercover work is a little rusty," she said, stroking him on the top of the head. "Let's go."

Liz walked away from the machine with Paddy, smiling to herself when she heard a kid squealing with delight as he scooped her winnings from the bottom of the machine.

As she walked back along the windy pier, she saw Adam and Mandy sitting on an iron bench. They were deep in conversation again. She almost wanted to walk over and sit by them, but she knew getting caught twice in one day was going to be more embarrassing than anything.

Deciding she had heard enough on her morning walk with Paddy, she headed back to her shop.

***

WHEN LIZ ARRIVED BACK AT THE SHOP, she was surprised to see someone looking through the window into the dark store. Liz approached, recognising the small woman as Laura, Frank's girlfriend.

Liz placed a hand on Laura's shoulder, making her jump out of her skin. She turned to face Liz, and it was obvious she had been recently crying. Her doe eyes were bright red, and she had small watery streaks of mascara trailing down each cheek.

"Are you ok?" Liz asked, regretting the question the second it left her lips. She knew it was a useless question to ask after having lost a loved one.

Laura opened her mouth to speak, but instead of words, she blubbered incoherently. Liz awkwardly embraced the short woman, and for a moment, she shared her grief as though her own was raw again.

"I'm sorry," Laura mumbled through the tears as Paddy began to yank on his lead. "You don't even know me. I don't know what you must think of me, it's just – I - *I loved* him."

Laura blubbered against Liz's jumper again, no doubt leaking mascara onto the fabric. Liz patted her back softly and looked down at Paddy.

"Do you want to come inside and talk?" Liz asked. "I'll make us some tea."

Laura pulled away and nodded. She wiped her

nose on the sleeve of her jacket and stepped back to let Liz unlock the shop door.

Once inside, Liz offered a box for Laura to sit on. She let Paddy off the lead before running upstairs to prepare the tea. When she returned, she was touched to see Paddy seated at Laura's feet.

"Frank loved this dog," Laura mumbled as she tickled behind his ears. "I always wondered if Paddy was the only one Frank truly loved."

"Christopher was going to send him to a shelter," Liz said. "We've become quite attached."

"Don't worry," Laura said with a strained laugh as she accepted the tea. "I'm not going to ask to keep him. He reminds me too much of – *well* –"

Laura's voice trailed off as she began to cry again. She looked down into the murky surface of her tea before taking a shaky sip.

"I'm afraid there isn't much here at the moment," Liz said, pulling up a box to sit on. "I'm still waiting for the stock and furniture deliveries. I couldn't get anything here sooner."

Laura looked around the bare shop, but she looked too exhausted to notice or care it was completely empty. She let out a long sigh as Paddy shuffled away from her to settle at Liz's feet.

"I thought he was being too nice to me," Laura chuckled forcefully. "He always preferred Frank, or maybe he just didn't like me. He seems quite content with you."

Liz looked down at Paddy, and even though they had only been together for a day, she felt like she had created a bond with the animal.

"I think he only likes me because I let him sleep on the bed," Liz offered. "I'm sure he misses Frank a lot."

Paddy looked up at Liz, his tongue poking out the side of his mouth, his eyes half closed. If the dog was grief-stricken, he was hiding it better than Laura.

"I know what everyone used to say behind my back," Laura said suddenly after a sip of tea. "I know they wouldn't have put me and Frank together. I wouldn't have either, until I got to know him." Laura paused and looked down into her tea, but she somehow managed to hold herself together. "Nobody knew him like I did. It just happened. People said he was a drunk, but he had a good reason."

"Do you mean because of his past?" Liz asked.

"You mean his dead wife?" Laura scoffed, almost sounding amused. "You *can* mention her. Frank's daughter, Mandy, made sure to remind me about her every chance she got, even if she didn't see her father very much. But to answer your question, Frank didn't drink because of his wife, it was something else entirely. It's not my place to say, even now, but knowing the gossips in this town, his secret will get out eventually. I just don't know what I'm going to do without him. Sure, we had our disagreements, but what couple doesn't?"

Liz rummaged in her handbag and passed Laura a tissue. She took it thankfully and blew her nose. Despite her curiosity, Liz decided not to push the subject further.

"My mum used to own this shop, ya'know," Laura said, looking around the store again. "It was a long time ago."

"Really?" Liz replied, her brows arching. "What was it?"

"A sweet shop," Laura said with a soft smile. "She used to bring me here on Saturdays when I was a little girl. My grandmother owned it before her, too. The supermarkets squeezed us out. She always thought I might take over one day, but it wasn't a viable business. We tried everything to keep it open, but loyalty is quite fickle when it comes to money around here. I'm just glad you've come to give it a new purpose. I heard you were opening a clothes shop?"

"Arts and crafts shop," Liz corrected her. "But close enough."

"That's how this place works," Laura said with a roll of her eyes. "It's one long game of Chinese whispers. I heard you used to be a police officer too."

"That part is true."

Laura looked at Liz suspiciously for a moment before blowing her nose on the tissue again.

"Well, either way, I'm glad you're going to be opening this old place," Laura said with a soft smile. "It's been empty for far too long. Bob Slinger has been trying to rent it out for a while, but nobody was interested."

"Well, I hope I can make your mother proud," Liz said, smiling at the woman.

"Me too," Laura replied, returning the smile. "I'm sure you will."

Laura's gaze wandered into the corner of the room where Liz had managed to display a few pieces of her work on easels in hopes it would pique the interest of passing locals. Most of them were paintings of the city. The biggest of them was a large canvas of a city skyline just before sunset, reds and purples licking the tops of the buildings, lights of offices dotting the structures. Laura stood up to take a closer look at the work.

"You painted these?" Laura asked.

"For my sins."

"They're really good," Laura said as she ran her fingers along the textured grooves of the oil paints. "You're very talented."

"Thank you," Liz said, feeling her cheeks blush a little. She had never been good at accepting compliments about her work.

"It's much better than that pompous, overpriced stuff they show at the gallery," Laura scoffed as she moved along the row of paintings. "It's supposed to be '*classic*', but it's not my cup of tea. You should ask if you can have some of your work displayed there. I can't tell you how much that gallery needs some real art."

"I'm not sure they're good enough to sell," Liz said sheepishly.

"Best art I've seen recently," Laura announced. "You have a real eye for colour and detail."

Liz thought about it for a moment, wondering if her work was good enough to be displayed in a gallery. It had been a dream of hers when she was younger and studying for her art degree in university, but lately she had settled on painting for her own enjoyment.

"I'll think about it," Liz said with a nod. "I've heard the owner is a bit scary."

"Katie Monroe?" Laura asked with a chuckle. "She might like to think she is, but she's just another rich toff who thinks she's better than the rest of us."

They both looked down at Paddy as he slept on his back on an old rug, his ears splayed out as he snored softly.

"Can I get you some more tea?" Liz asked as she looked down at Laura's empty cup.

"I should get going," she said, her air of sadness returning. "I suppose I should face the funeral plans. Thanks for taking my mind off things."

Liz followed Laura to the door and held it open

for her. Liz liked to think their ten minutes together had provided a little distraction from her grief.

"I think you will make my mum proud," Laura said with a firm nod as she looked up at the building. "You're a good woman."

Laura turned on her heels, dropped her head, and hurried down the street and out of sight. Liz called for Paddy, who jumped up and scurried towards her. She locked up the shop and opened her flat door. Paddy ran upstairs as soon as it was open, but Liz paused and looked around the square. She had never expected to be so integrated so quickly, but it was becoming increasingly more difficult to remember a life before Scarlet Cove.

Just as she turned back to her door, she spotted Simon walking past the Fish and Anchor with Ellie skipping happily by his side. Simon waved in her direction, flashing his dimpled smile. She felt a familiar squirming in her stomach as she waved back.

Six

Liz looked wearily out of the shop window, rubbing the sleep from her eyes. She caught her reflection in the window as she watched the deliverymen unload the boxes of flat pack furniture off the back of the van. Her hair was a mess of red frizz, and her eyes were half-closed. Her mind was still asleep after being awoken by the buzzer minutes earlier. She tucked her messy hair behind her ears and held the door open, smiling meekly at the men as they carried the giant boxes into the empty shop.

When they were done, Liz handed them a generous tip for not asking her to help. She stepped back and looked at the furniture, her heart sinking to the pit of her stomach. She still had Bob Slinger's electric drill, but she was not going to be able to assemble everything herself. With a cheeky smile, she pulled her phone from her pocket and scrolled through her recently added contacts.

***

"WELL, FIRST THINGS FIRST, WE NEED TO make some room," Nancy announced as she scratched at the messy bun on top of her head. "Is all of this even going to fit in this tiny shop?"

"Maybe I read the measurements wrong," Liz mumbled as she looked down at the pile of giant boxes. "Or Bob Slinger measured the shop incorrectly?"

"He has *impeccable* eyesight," Nancy announced without irony. "He's been asked to be the judge of the tug-of-war contest at the Scarlet Cove summer fair for –"

"As long as anyone can remember?"

"How do you do that?" Nancy giggled with a shake of her head. "Are you sure you've made the right decision quitting the police? You're *quite* intuitive."

"It's a gift," Liz replied with a smirk.

Liz used her keys to rip open the tape on the first box. She peered inside, instantly recognising it as the distressed eggshell blue shelves she had painstakingly picked out from the catalogue.

"I think I want this next to the entrance on the right," Liz said, resting her keys against her lips as she looked at the blank wall. "It will look nice with paints on it, so they're the first things you see when you walk in."

They dragged the large box over to the spot near the door before assembling it using Bob Slinger's drill. To Liz's surprise, Nancy was quite adept at reading flat pack instructions, meaning the shelves were built quicker than Liz would have managed alone.

"That wasn't so hard," Liz said stepping back to admire their handiwork. "Was it?"

"My hands are killing me," Nancy exhaled, rubbing her red palms together. "Couldn't you have bought preassembled furniture?

"It's more expensive," Liz replied with a shrug. "There should be a matching counter somewhere."

They wandered back over to the pile of boxes. Liz quickly realised each of the boxes had a label listing its contents, taking the guesswork out of things.

"Found it!" Nancy exclaimed. "Oh, dear. This box is even bigger."

They dragged the box away from the pile, a smaller box tumbling over, sending up a cloud of dust as it hit the floor.

"I want this in front of the storeroom door," Liz wheezed as they dragged the large box. "Makes sense, right?"

"I've never opened a shop," Nancy replied through tight lips. "Maybe my Jack would have been better. Or maybe you could have asked Simon?"

"Why would I ask Simon?" Liz asked, arching a brow when the box was finally where she wanted it. "I barely know him."

"Oh, I don't know about that." Nancy placed

her hands on the small of her back and stretched out. "I think you two got on quite well at the pub the other day."

"I don't need you to play cupid," Liz retorted as she dragged the keys across the box. "Have you heard anything else about Frank?"

"Since you last asked?" Nancy asked, with raised eyebrows as she pulled a blue wooden leg out of the box. "Nothing new, no. People 'round here are happy to put it down to a drunken mistake."

Liz thought about that for a moment, but it just did not make sense, no matter how hard she tried to believe it.

"Does that sound right to you?" Liz asked. "A man of reasonable health getting drunk and accidentally killing himself on a fishing boat he's worked on for as long as anyone can remember?"

"Accidents *do* happen," Nancy said as she read over the instructions. "This one looks so much harder."

"Something just doesn't sit right with me," Liz mumbled, almost to herself. "I was at the pier yesterday, and I saw Adam, that apprentice he fired in front of us, with Mandy from the pub. I think they're in a relationship."

"A relationship?" Nancy asked, her jaw dropping, a smile tickling the corners of her lips. "I *knew* it! Nothing stays secret in Scarlet Cove."

"Everyone seems to be saying that," Liz replied, taking one side of the counter top as Nancy took the other, placing it on the legs. "And yet it seems the truth surrounding Frank's death is so secret it's sunk to the bottom of the sea, just like he would have done without his lifejacket."

"Folk in Scarlet Cove love to gossip," Nancy said, almost defensively. "Nothing else happens here. Aside from our new redheaded retired detective, it's usually trivial stuff."

"So, everyone gets involved in everyone else's business then?"

"We take a *mild* interest," Nancy replied with a grin. "It's boring here! I spend all of my time at the gallery, and when I'm not there, I'm with Jack, but there's nothing to do here. There's no nightclub or cinema. You've got Coastline Cabaret, which is full of old folks, and the Fish and Anchor. Gossiping is all we have."

Liz thought back to what Miles, her detective

friend from Manchester, had said to her before they had parted ways. He had handed her a cactus, and told her that people in small towns were worse than those in the city. Had he been talking about the murder, the gossip, or both?

"There's quite an age gap between Mandy and Adam," Liz said as she sorted out the screws into piles. "He looks like a child."

"There isn't much choice 'round here," Nancy reminded her. "It's a small dating pool. I've known Jack since school, but we only got together last year. Not everyone is that lucky. Mandy divorced her husband, or should I say, he divorced her. She married rich, obviously. Women like her usually do. It backfired. He saw right through her. I guess she decided to pick someone younger. Maybe she's reliving her youth? I think she's only twenty-seven, but the cake on her face ages her."

As they worked on the counter, Liz tried to think of the types of conversations a twenty-seven-year-old woman could have with a nineteen-year-old boy. No matter how much she tried, she could not imagine their relationship being anything more than physical. They were both attractive people, but she would have thought Mandy was his auntie or older sister if she had seen them out in public and not seen how intimate they were.

The remainder of the boxes were significantly smaller, and it was not long before they had the rest of them made up. While Nancy made them cups of tea in the flat upstairs, Liz got to work unloading her stock and putting everything where she wanted it. When she was done, she stepped back and planted her hands on her hips, pleased with the placement of the arts and crafts supplies.

"What do you think?" Liz asked when Nancy pushed through the front door with two cups of tea. "Look like an arts and crafts shop to you?"

"Oh, Liz!" Nancy exclaimed, grinning from ear to ear. "It looks *exactly* like an arts and crafts shop! Makes me wish I could use the stuff."

"I couldn't have done it without you."

"That's what friends are for, right?" Nancy said with a wink as she handed over the cup of tea. "You can buy me a drink sometime to say thank you."

Before Liz could agree that the proposal seemed like a fair deal, Nancy's phone rang, causing her to pass her hot cup to Liz and dive for her pocket. The smile on her face told Liz exactly who it was.

"It's Jack," Nancy said, resting the phone against her chest. "I should take this."

Leaving Nancy to her conversation, Liz took her cup of tea up to the flat and looked around her new home. Paddy peered up at her from his position on the couch, but he was too comfortable to move. She could hardly believe her dream was coming together, and without much of a hitch. She cast an eye to the cactus that Miles had given her, which she had affectionately named Spiky. Her friend would not even recognise her if he saw her now. She could not even remember how many days it had been since she had left Manchester. Had it been a week or a month? Either way, it felt like Scarlet Cove was exactly where she should be.

"*Liz!*" Nancy's scream called from the shop below. "*Liz – I think – you should – get down here.*"

Liz ditched her tea next to the cactus on the TV stand and took the stairs down to the street two at a time. Even through the shop window, she could see exactly what had caused Nancy to scream. Water sprayed wildly from the storeroom behind the counter, soaking her shop.

"What happened?" Liz cried as she burst through the door. "My shop!"

"I don't know," Nancy cried, soaked from head to toe as she held her hands up to stop the spray of water. "I was on the phone to Jack when I heard something pop, and the next thing I know I was being attacked by water."

Before Liz could do anything to stop the flow, the shop door opened, making both women spin, the burst pipe continuing to soak them.

"Is everything okay?" Christopher asked breathlessly as he ran into the shop. "I heard Nancy from the market. I thought someone was hurt."

The water flow turned from a stream to a gentle spray. Nancy and Liz looked at each other, immediately bursting into a fit of laughter.

"We're fine" Nancy giggled. "I think a pipe burst. It's an old shop."

Christopher followed them into the storeroom. The pipe had forced through the plaster and was now only dribbling as the water tank emptied.

"I'm not much of a plumber," Christopher said as he sucked the air through his teeth. "Looks like the welding has weakened and snapped. It's probably not accustomed to being used. This place has been empty for quite a while."

Nancy glanced at Liz and playfully rolled her eyes as Christopher ran his finger along the rim of the jagged copper pipe.

"I have the number for someone who can fix it," Christopher said, already pulling his phone out. "He owes me a favour. Mention my name. I'm sure he'll give you a discount."

Christopher pulled a small notepad and a pen from his inner jacket pocket and quickly scribbled down the number. He handed it over with a toothy smile. Liz looked down at it, almost reluctant to take it. She hated ever feeling like a damsel in distress, but she knew she did not have a leg to stand on, especially since she was dripping wet.

"I hope he's not a cowboy," Liz said, accepting the piece of paper.

"Only the best for you," Christopher said, his minty breath hitting her face. "I only associate with the best, Elizabeth."

"I should go," Nancy announced, grinning at Liz as she squeezed through them. "Jack wants to meet for dinner, and I think I need a change of clothes."

Liz pleaded with her friend with her eyes not to leave them alone, but Nancy smirked as she gently hugged Liz. Nancy knew exactly what she was doing, and Liz did not need to be a detective to see through it.

"Let's step outside," Christopher said, glancing at the pipe again. "I don't want to get this suit wet. It *was* rather expensive."

Liz rolled her eyes and walked out of the small storeroom. Christopher placed his hand on the small of her back, guiding her to the door. It was not until they were out on the street that she realised she did not like it, and jerked out of the way, leaving Christopher to awkwardly drop his arms to his side.

"Have you visited The Sea Platter yet?" he asked after a prolonged period of silence. "They have the best fish, mainly because I deliver to them."

"Not yet," she said quickly "I've been really busy."

"Let me invite you to dinner," he announced firmly. "They always reserve a table for me."

The invitation took Liz by surprise. She thought for a moment for a way to let him down gently, especially since he had just given her the number for a plumber, but the thought of having another microwavable meal turned her stomach. It would be nice to have something fresh for once, and she did not doubt Christopher would pay.

"It's on my list of places to visit," Liz thought aloud. "I do really need to get a plumber out here though. I can't live without water."

"*Perfect!*" Christopher announced, taking her vague response as confirmation. "I'll meet you at eight. Hopefully, you'll have dried off before then."

Christopher bowed his head, turned on his heels, and marched across the road and through the market without another word.

"See you later," Liz mumbled to herself, before sighing and looking back at her soaked shop. "Without a hitch, right? *Ha!*"

Seven

Standing outside The Sea Platter, Liz pulled her cardigan tighter around her shoulders as the cool breeze swept down the seafront. She inhaled the fresh salty air, wondering if she would ever tire of the smell.

She checked her watch. Christopher was not late, but she was early. It had always been a habit to arrive everywhere ten minutes early, something her parents had drilled into her at a young age. They were polite to a fault and so proper she knew they would be outraged if they saw that Liz was only wearing jeans, a simple t-shirt, and a thin cardigan to have dinner with a man. They would practically keel over and die if they found out the man in question was single.

She crossed the road and leaned against the sea wall. The lights of the businesses on the seafront illuminated the waves as they crashed below, but when she looked out to the horizon, she could not tell where the sea ended and the sky began; it was how she liked it. She was on the edge of the country, and the only way to look was forward.

She turned at the sound of a car's engine. She wondered if it might be Christopher, but she was surprised to see Simon climb out of the car. His dimples sprung out when he noticed her standing by the wall.

"Liz!" he cried cheerfully as he walked around the car to open the boot. "Out for a late night stroll?"

She looked at the small restaurant, which already packed out, except for one table. Without knowing why, she found she did not want to tell Simon the real reason she was there.

"I'm meeting someone for dinner," she said casually. "Are you eating here too?"

"I'm just delivering some ice cream," he said as he pulled a crate out of the back of the car. "They've run out of the vanilla so they asked if I could run down with some."

"It sounds like you're never off the clock."

"I don't mind," he said with a small shrug. "When duty calls, I listen."

He flashed her a quick smile before heading into the restaurant with the ice cream. The chatter from the patrons flooded out as they enjoyed their food and wine. Liz began to wonder why she had accepted Christopher's offer of dinner. She looked down the street and wondered if she could slip home and feign illness, but her heart sank when she saw Christopher walking towards her in a tuxedo, carrying a large bouquet of blood-red roses.

"You're here," he said, almost a little surprised. "*For you.*"

She clumsily accepted the flowers, inhaling their fresh scent. Lewis had always bought her red roses too.

"They're beautiful," Liz said as she looked over Christopher's smart tuxedo. "Maybe a little unnecessary though."

"*Nonsense!*" he exclaimed, clapping his hands together and sending his sharp, strong aftershave in Liz's direction. "I wouldn't be being true to myself if I wasn't a gentleman on a date."

"This isn't a date," she reminded him. "We're just two friends, having dinner."

The restaurant door opened and Simon walked out, looking over his shoulder as he said his goodbyes to the owner. He turned around, his eyes darting from the roses, to Christopher, and then to Liz. His smile instantly vanished.

"Chris," Simon said with a curt nod. "*Evening.*"

"It's Chris*topher*, Simon," he replied with a strained smile. "You should know that by now. On your rounds?"

"They ran out of ice cream," Simon said, his brows creasing together as he hooked his thumb over his shoulder. "Are you two on a date?"

"No," Liz replied quickly.

"Of sorts," Christopher said, edging in and

putting his arm around Liz's shoulder. "I saved Elizabeth from a spot of bother with a burst pipe, and she accepted my invitation to dinner."

"As *friends*," she corrected him, looking down at the roses, her shoulder burning under his hand.

Simon nodded curtly, a sad smile on his face as he stared at Liz. Liz did not want to admit he looked entirely disappointed by her choice of company for dinner.

"Looks like a date to me," he said with a forced smile. "Enjoy your dinner."

"We will," Christopher exclaimed as he pulled Liz in even tighter. "Can't wait to have your ice cream for dessert."

Simon jumped into his car, slammed the door, and sped down the seafront. Liz wriggled out of Christopher's grip and dropped the roses to her side. She knew it would not be long before the whole town was talking about her date with Fishy Chris, and she knew no amount of denial would change that it was a date.

Knowing there was no turning back, Liz followed Christopher into the restaurant. Most of the customers nodded their acknowledgement of

Christopher as he strode through the restaurant. Those same people gave Liz a curious look, their eyes widening when they saw the roses.

"*Daniel*." Christopher exclaimed as he slapped his hand into that of a smartly dressed man. "Daniel Clark, I'd like you to meet Elizabeth Jones."

"You must be our new resident," Daniel said as he heartily accepted her hand. "Welcome to Scarlet Cove, Elizabeth."

"Thank you," she said. "People usually call me Liz."

"Right this way, Liz," Daniel said as he led them across the restaurant. "When I knew Christopher was coming down for dinner, I made sure to save the best seats in the house for you."

He showed them to a small table in the window of the restaurant. The candles were already lit, and there was already a single rose sitting in a tall glass in the centre of the frilly white tablecloth. Liz wondered if every customer got such treatment when they came for dinner.

Liz sat down, the observers making her a little uncomfortable. She propped the roses on the floor against the table leg, and quickly blew out the candle as she sat down.

"I hope you like seafood," Christopher said, staring with an arched brow at the smoking wick. "Daniel is the best chef on the whole South Coast, and it doesn't hurt that he gets the best fish delivered daily."

"It takes the best to make the best," Daniel said as he slapped Christopher on the shoulder. "Can I get you some wine?"

"Yes," Liz answered quickly.

"We'll take a bottle of the *Châteauneuf du Pape*," Christopher said without needing to look at the menu, his tongue rolling around the letters expertly. "And some oysters to start."

Daniel scribbled down their order in the pad before scurrying off. Liz was ashamed to say she had never tried oysters or Châteauneuf du Pape. Her wine taste was narrowed down to whatever was on offer at the supermarket, and she was more interested in a fish finger sandwich than slurping an oyster out of a shell.

"You speak French?" she asked as she glanced over the extensive menu of seafood.

"*Oui. Je parle couramment le français,*" he

announced confidently as he unbuttoned the jacket of his tuxedo. "I had the finest education money could buy."

Liz looked down at the menu again, wondering if that was a brag, or if he was just stating a fact. It only confirmed her suspicions about Christopher being wealthy.

"What about you?"

"What about me?" she asked.

"Your education," he said with a sly smile. "A woman as confident and feisty as you must be well educated."

Something about the way Christopher said '*feisty*' made her wonder if it was a compliment or an insult.

"I went to a normal primary school in Manchester, and the local comprehensive," she said. "I got okay grades when I left school, but I failed French."

"It *is* very difficult," Christopher said with a nod. "Although *I* picked it up quite easily."

Liz widened her eyes as she looked back at the menu. She was glad it was not an official date because if it was, it would not be going well. She wondered if Christopher could even hear himself talking sometimes.

"No university education?" he asked.

"I have a first class degree in fine art from the Manchester Metropolitan University. Although that feels like a lifetime ago now. My parents wanted me to study law, but it never interested me."

"Ah, law," Christopher cried enthusiastically. "Now *that* is a solid profession."

"You sound just like my parents," she said with an uneasy smile. "They're both lawyers. They wanted me to follow in their footsteps, but it was never my calling."

"So, you followed a career into the arts?" he asked, raising a brow slightly. "How rebellious of you."

"Actually, my career took me into the police force," she replied, feeling herself getting increasingly irritated by his tone. "I was in the Greater Manchester Police for fifteen years."

Christopher's head recoiled a little, his toothy smile growing wider as his eyes narrowed curiously.

"A lady police officer?" he replied with an amused smile. "I would never have guessed."

"I was a detective," she said, her tone flat and her lips not returning his smile. "That's all in the past now."

"Why would you leave such an honoured rank?"

Liz opened her mouth to reply, unsure of what she was going to say, glad when she saw Daniel hurrying across the restaurant with a bottle of wine. She suddenly sat up straight and smiled at the owner as he approached Christopher with a look she was sure was terror.

He opened the bottle and poured a little sample into the glass. Christopher swirled it around under his nose before slurping a little. He swished it around in his mouth for what felt like a lifetime before he nodded. Daniel let out a relieved laugh as he filled up their two glasses.

"*Oysters!*" Daniel exclaimed after hurrying back with a silver tray. "Give me a shout when you're ready to order your main course."

Liz thanked him with a smile before looking down at the tray of oysters, which had been served with lemons and mignonette sauce. Her stomach turned at the thought of them, but up close, their slimy bodies looked even less appetising in their dark grey shells.

"Do you like oysters?" Christopher asked after picking one up and slurping it down in one gulp. "If I could eat them every day, I would."

"I can't say I've ever had the privilege," Liz mumbled as she poked the soft middle with her knife.

"Pick it up, lift it to your lips, give it a little chew, and then swallow," Christopher said before repeating the action. "I only farm and harvest the *finest* oysters."

Liz picked up the shell, unsure of how her evening had taken this turn. She thought about her freezer full of microwave meals at the flat, and they suddenly did not seem so unpalatable.

"*Cheers*," she said with a tip of her head as she lifted it to her lips.

As instructed, she tossed the oyster and its slimy liquid into her mouth. She chewed the body a couple of times, which had the consistency of an overcooked boiled egg. She quickly swallowed it and placed the shell back on the tray.

"Well?" Christopher said, edging forward across the table. "Aren't they delicious? They're aphrodisiacs, you know."

"They taste like the ocean," Liz said as she rubbed her tongue against her palette. "I'm not sure if they're for me."

"Maybe they just take some getting used to. I've had them since I was a child, so I've always liked them."

"What kind of child eats oysters?" she asked with a chuckle.

"A Monroe child," he replied seriously. "When you're surrounded by as many cooks, nannies, and private tutors as money can buy, you find you gain an appreciation for the finer things in life."

"Sounds like you had a busy upbringing."

"It was incredibly lonely."

Christopher's expression dropped, the veneer sliding away for the first time since Liz had met him. It bounced back in a moment, and after a sip of wine and another oyster, he was back grinning at her like a deranged puppet.

"Were you an only child?" she asked.

"I have a sister," Christopher said. "I think when my parents had one of each, they decided they had the perfect family on paper, not that they were around much."

"That sounds so sad."

"It wasn't for them," he said vacantly as he picked up another oyster. "Skiing in Aspen, cruises around the Caribbean, safaris in the Serengeti. They did it all and saw it all, while we were –"

"At home in the mansion with the nanny?"

"You guessed it," he said with a sad chuckle. "Enough about me. What about you? It must have been interesting growing up with lawyers as parents?"

"Interesting is *one* word for it," Liz said as she reached out for the wine glass, something that had become a habit whenever she talked about her parents. "I felt like a constant disappointment. They hated me wanting to be an artist, and they hated me even more when I wanted to be a police officer. I think that made me want to do it even more. They got what they wanted with my little sister, Lacey, though. She followed them into law. She's a top environmental lawyer in London. I think she's happy, so that's all that matters."

"And now you're about to open your own shop," Christopher said, tipping his glass to her.

"That's something to be proud of."

"I suppose it is."

He chinked his glass against hers and shot her a smile that almost made him seem human. She had not thought much about her parents when it came to the shop. She had only told them when it was too late to back out of anything, not that they would have tried to stop her. They had given up trying to mould her life a long time ago. They had not agreed with her career, or her marriage, so she knew they were not about to agree with her running away to the coast to pursue her passion.

When they were finished with the oysters, Daniel returned to take their orders. Christopher ordered grilled salmon with buttered asparagus and garlic new potatoes, but Liz kept it safe and ordered fish and chips, which caused Christopher to arch his brows again.

"Can you believe I've moved to the coast and I haven't had any fish and chips yet?" she said, almost defensively. "It's almost criminal."

"You've been busy putting together your shop and getting drenched in water from burst pipes," Christopher reminded her. "Did you call the plumber?"

"He was around within the hour when I mentioned your name, and Bob said he'll cover the costs, so there's no harm done."

"It's nice to know the Monroe name still carries weight in this town," Christopher said proudly. "Even if it is just my sister and I now."

"Oh, I'm so sorry."

"They're not dead," he said quickly. "My mother and father retired to Australia a decade ago. I haven't seen them since, but they call once a month to check if I'm married yet."

Christopher sipped his wine as though that was a normal conversation to have with one's parents when they were halfway across the globe. Liz's parents called as often, but they usually kept their conversation to trivial matters to avoid arguments.

"I'm sure they're proud of you running your fishing business," Liz suggested, as she looked around the full restaurant, glad that interest in her presence had subsided. "From what I've heard, you've built quite an empire."

"They think working is common. They gave me enough money in my trust fund to never need to work again, but I always enjoyed fishing, so I bought the business when it came up for sale."

"Did Frank come as part of that deal?" Liz asked, eager to find out even more about the dead fisher. "I heard the men in his family had been fishers for generations."

"I got Frank and his father when I took over things. They were great at what they did, but they didn't share my vision. They didn't think the business could be any bigger than it was, but I always saw the bigger picture. Things got easier when Frank's dad died about eight years ago. Frank didn't kick up too much of a fuss when I started to change things and hire more people. I think he liked it just being him, but I promoted him to head fisher to soothe his ego. It wasn't a real title, but I let him choose who he hired and fired. The thing about Frank was that he was very particular about who he worked with. Adam was the latest in a long line of failed apprentices, which was why I wasn't surprised when he fired him the day before – *well*, you know what happened next."

"I heard that Adam and Mandy might have been having a love affair?"

Christopher smirked as he sipped his wine. Daniel hurried over with their food and left them to eat in peace.

"You're fitting into Scarlet Cove quite well, I see," Christopher said as he cut his asparagus. "Adam is a child, and Mandy wanted to get at her father. She's a beautiful girl, but she's difficult. It had the desired effect and drove her father to his death."

"You think Mandy was only with Adam to wind her father up?"

"What else could a twenty-seven-year-old see in a nineteen-year-old boy?" Christopher paused to put a tiny piece of salmon into his mouth, which he chewed slowly and delicately before continuing. "Adam was like the son Frank never had. I think Frank felt betrayed, but who's to know what the man was thinking when he decided to get drunk at work."

"You still think it was an accident?"

"You don't, Detective?" Christopher asked with a small roll of his eyes. "The only suspicious thing here is that Frank was drinking on the job. I should have fired him months ago. He was getting worse and worse. It was a blessing in disguise. I can hire someone competent to do his job now."

Liz tossed a chip into her mouth, wondering how Christopher could be so cold about the death of a staff member. Even she was not being that detached, despite not knowing the man. They ate the rest of their food in silence, which seemed to suit Christopher. He kept his elbows off the table, did not talk with his mouth full, and wiped his lips in between each mouthful. She wondered how he could have the energy to make eating look so uptight.

When Liz finished, she leaned back in her chair as she pushed her food away. As fish and chips went, it was probably the best she had experienced. The fish had been perfectly flaky, the batter rich and crispy, and the chips had been fried so delicately that they remained fluffy beyond their golden crunchy exteriors. Topped off with a healthy dose of salt and vinegar and good wine, it was the perfect fish and chip supper.

Liz stared out of the window at the moonlight's reflection on the surface of the dark sea, knowing there was nowhere else she was going to get fish as fresh as here. Even though she did not take many risks with her food, she would like to think she could make her way through the rest of the menu to see what Scarlet Cove really had to offer.

Liz was about to ask Christopher what he recommended she try next, if only to keep the conversation flowing until dessert, but a scuffle at the bar in the corner caught her attention, as well as that of everyone else in the restaurant.

Liz watched as Daniel tried to steady the drunken man, who looked like he was refusing to leave. Her police training kicked in right away, and she had to force herself to hold onto her seat rather than rush over and make a fool of herself.

The man fell off his stool and turned to face the restaurant with blurry eyes. Even behind his drunken state, she could tell he was embarrassed. Liz recognised the man as the one she had seen Laura speaking to outside the cabaret bar during her walk down to the harbour.

"Is that Michael?" Liz asked.

Christopher stopped checking his teeth in the reflection of his knife. He turned awkwardly in his chair to glance at the bar in the corner.

"Poor man," Christopher said with a nod as he

turned back. "Must have been kicked out of the Fish and Anchor."

"Does he drink a lot?" Liz asked.

"Only since Laura left him."

"I thought they were still friends?"

"That's what Laura wants to think," Christopher said with a small shrug. "I think it makes her feel a little better about dumping him for Frank. He makes sure she never sees him like this, but word must get back to her."

Liz watched as Michael stumbled to the door, slurring his apologies to everyone in his line of sight.

"Quite improper," Christopher said with a shake of his head.

The rest of the meal went by without incident. They had dessert, and despite Liz assuming Christopher would pay, which he tried to, she insisted on paying half.

After a small walk along the seafront, they headed up the twisting and winding narrow streets towards Liz's shop. They barely spoke a word to each other.

"Thank you for the roses," Liz said, knowing it was the polite thing to say. "They're lovely."

Christopher smiled down at her. He suddenly closed his eyes and leaned in, his lips pursed. As soon as Liz realised his intentions, she turned her head and inhaled the roses again, his lips brushing awkwardly against her ear.

She watched as Christopher opened his eyes, and she had to face his obvious embarrassment at being rejected.

"I'll see you later," Liz said quietly, pulling her keys from her jeans pocket. "Thanks for dinner."

Before Christopher could say another word, she slipped into her flat, locking the door behind her. She dropped the roses to her side and rested her head against the door. She let out an exhausted sigh, having felt like she had been holding her breath for most of the night. She heard a similar sigh coming from the other side of the door.

Eight

With a collection of her best work under her arm, Liz set off to Nancy's gallery the next morning. She walked into the foyer, pleased the first face she saw was Nancy's, sitting behind a mahogany desk. An antique green lamp and a bromeliad plant in an orange plant pot decorated her workspace.

"*Liz!*" Nancy beamed, jumping out of her seat

and closing the magazine she had been reading. "What a nice surprise! What are you doing here?"

"I thought I'd show some of my work to the owner." Liz nodded awkwardly to the canvases under her arm, suddenly unsure about how she had chosen to spend her morning. "My work has never been shown in a gallery, but I thought it was worth a shot."

"The dragon is busy showing some dealers around," Nancy whispered, glancing down the oak corridor. "She should be done soon. Can I have a look? You haven't shown me what you can do yet."

Liz gripped the paintings closer to her body. It was not that she did not want to show Nancy her work, but her painting had been a private thing for so long, it felt weird to show someone she considered a friend. Nobody at the station had known she painted, except for Miles, who had always approached her passion with mild curiosity.

"I guess so," Liz said with a nervous smile. "I'm no Van Gogh."

Nancy darted around her desk, glancing down the corridor again. She held her hand out, so Liz selected one at random. Nancy looked down at the painting with a tilted head, her silent observation unsettling Liz.

"You're far too modest," Nancy beamed, holding the painting of a forest at arm's length. "This is really great. You clearly have a talent. Why don't you have a wander? You might bump into the dragon on your way around."

Liz left Nancy to her magazine. She took herself and her paintings down the corridor and into the main gallery. She did not know what she had expected from a gallery in Scarlet Cove, but this was not it. The floor was made completely of white marble, which glittered under the domed skylight in the ceiling. The white walls stretched up high, down-lit paintings in gold frames scattering the walls. Liz looked down at her own work, which was nowhere near as classical in style as the stuffy oil paintings she was faced with.

"Can I help you?" a stern voice asked, dragging Liz away from the painting she had been inspecting.

Liz turned to see a smart looking woman with strikingly blonde hair scraped back into a bun. Her grey eyes blazed against her naturally bronzed skin, which was free of makeup, but was so taut and smooth it did not need any. She was wearing a pressed white blouse, which was tucked into a calf-length pencil skirt, and finished off with black stilettos. She towered over Liz, who was used to being the tallest in the room.

"I'm Liz," she said, not as intimidated by the woman as much as she suspected she should have been. "I've just moved here. You might have heard? I'm opening an arts and crafts shop."

"I haven't heard anything," she said with a subtle arch of her neat brows.

"I think you're the first person to say that," Liz said, forcing a laugh, hoping to lighten the mood, but the woman's face did not crack. "I'm an artist, and I thought I'd drop by and show you some of my work."

"Why would you do that?"

"Because this is a gallery."

The woman huffed and rolled her eyes, glancing at the stack of canvases under Liz's arm. She suddenly moved them back, regretting her decision to turn up unsolicited.

"I suppose you should follow me," the woman said with a strained smile, turning on her heels and marching back the way she had come. "Quickly. I haven't got all day."

Liz hurried after the woman, now knowing why Nancy constantly referred to her boss as '*the dragon*'.

She followed the woman down the corridor, jogging to keep up. She made walking in a pencil skirt and heels look easy. Even at the station, Liz had always opted for trousers and flat shoes. She had never understood why women tortured themselves by choosing style over comfort.

They reached a door labelled '*Katelyn Monroe – Gallery Manager*'. Liz wondered how common the Monroe name was in Scarlet Cove.

"Are you any relation of Chris Monroe?" Liz asked as she followed the woman into her office.

"You mean Chris*topher*?" she snapped, glancing over her shoulder as she marched over to her desk. "He's my brother."

"That makes sense," Liz mumbled under her breath as she looked around the ornately decorated office, which looked like an extension of the gallery.

Katelyn sat behind the desk and pulled a pair of delicate spectacles out of a box. She flicked on the green lamp, which matched the one on Nancy's desk, and held her hand out as she stared over her glasses at Liz. The woman could not have looked more disinterested if she tried.

"I don't usually look at uninvited work," Katelyn said as she snapped her perfectly manicured fingers together.

"Thank you?" Liz said, unsure if she should be grateful.

Sensing Katelyn's growing irritation, Liz propped her paintings against the desk and selected two of her favourite pieces. The first was a skyline of Manchester she had painted in her final days living in the city, and the second was the painting of the sea she had started before finding Frank's body and finished later at her flat. She was not sure if these were her best pieces, but she liked the contrast of the grey city next to the bright sky.

"I have more," Liz said, her eyes trained on Katelyn's icy expression. "These are just some of-"

Katelyn silenced Liz with a finger, her eyes trained on Liz's brush strokes.

"I'm afraid it's not the kind of work we display here at Scarlet Cove Gallery," Katelyn said, pulling her glasses off and giving Liz a look she knew was to let her know she had wasted her precious time. "You could always ask the café."

Liz opened her mouth to speak, but she did not know what to say. It took a lot for another person to render Liz speechless, especially after so many years working as a detective, but as she stared at the disinterested gallery owner, she realised this was one of those rare occasions.

"I suppose you're the woman who went on a date with my brother last night?" Katelyn asked, mild amusement in her stony voice. "Unless there is another red-headed Elizabeth in town?"

Liz opened her mouth to speak again, but no words came out. Had Katelyn known exactly who she was from the moment she had seen her?

"It wasn't a date," Liz mumbled feebly.

"I'm quite busy, Elizabeth," Katelyn said, grabbing her glasses again before looking down at the paperwork on her desk. "Close the door on your way out."

Completely dumbfounded, Liz stared at the woman for a moment, before scooping up her paintings and heading for the door. With her paintings under her arm, she stayed outside for a moment, wanting to march right back in to give the pretentious manager a piece of her mind. Liz had not expected to have her work on the walls by the end of the day, but she had not expected such a verbal lashing from a woman she thought might be at least interested in discussing art.

With her tail between her legs, Liz hurried down the corridor, not wanting Nancy to see her with an embarrassed look on her face.

"*Liz!*" Nancy called after her as Liz headed for the door. "What happened?"

"Nothing," Liz said, stopping in her tracks to face her friend as she scurried around her desk. "I'm fine."

"You don't look fine," Nancy said soothingly, rubbing Liz's arms. "What did she say to you?"

"She hated my work," Liz said, glancing down at the paintings, wondering if they were better suited to the bin than a gallery's walls. "How do you work for someone like that?"

"I try to stay out of her way," Nancy shrugged. "I just love being surrounded by the art. It's the only thing keeping me here. For what it's worth, I love your style. Katelyn wouldn't know real art if it hit her in the face. She only likes the classics. Once your shop opens, everyone will see how great you are."

"I don't know about that," Liz said, feeling her cheeks blushing. "I'll see you later. I was going to pop into the salon. I've not had my hair trimmed in what feels like a lifetime."

Liz walked out of the stuffy gallery, the fresh air relaxing her. She smiled up at the sun, promising nothing was going to ruin her mood. If Katelyn hated her work, she would just have to up her game and paint something better.

Liz set off down the street, following behind two elderly women who were talking in whispers. It was not a habit of hers to eavesdrop on strangers, but their conversation instantly pricked up her ears.

"*Poison*, you say?" one of the women mumbled, gasping dramatically. "*Who* would have done such a thing to poor Frank?"

"It's just *terrible* isn't it, Sylvia?" the other lady replied. "It's *quite* the scandal. I heard from my Bobby whose girlfriend works at the station. They're going to announce it any day now, but I think they're scared of spooking the killer."

"A *murder* in Scarlet Cove?" the other woman

said. "*Quite* the scandal *indeed.*"

Both of the women slipped into Driftwood Café, leaving Liz on the corner of her shop's street. She allowed herself to smile for a moment for being right about it being murder, but it quickly dropped when she realised the murderer was still out there.

After dropping her paintings in her shop, Liz set off towards the hair salon, knowing she would never book herself in if she put it off any longer.

***

"YOUR HAIR COLOUR IS GORGEOUS, babe," Polly Spragg, the owner of Crazy Waves, announced in her thick Essex accent. "Is it natural?"

"This is just how it grows," Liz replied, assessing her bushy red locks in the mirror.

"Wish I could pull this colour off." Polly leaned over and dragged Liz's long curls across her forehead. "I don't have the complexion. Too tanned. I'd look like a carrot, wouldn't I, babe?"

Polly tossed her head back and cackled, following it with a deep snort. She looked quite young, her peroxide blonde beehive and glowing orange tan both as unnatural as each other. Her makeup was too thick, her clothes too tight, and her heels too high, but Liz decided she liked her. She wore her personality like a badge of honour, and Liz found something quite pure about that.

After a minute of back and forth, Liz agreed to have her hair straightened so Polly could achieve the best cut.

"I heard about your dad, babe," Polly announced. "Must be awful for you."

Liz looked under her hair and into the mirror, suddenly noticing that Mandy was behind her having her nails done at a little white desk. Mandy looked up from her phone with a blank expression. She forced a smile in Polly's direction, but she did not seem all that grief stricken.

Liz was so focussed on watching Mandy in the mirror, she did not notice that Polly had finished straightening her hair. When she looked up, she barely recognised her reflection.

"You look gorgeous, babe!" Polly beamed, clapping her tanned hands together. "You should wear it straight more! It suits you."

Liz turned her head, unsure of what she

thought. She had once straightened her hair for her sister's wedding, but she had convinced herself it did not suit her, and had never reattempted it. She wondered if Polly was an exceptionally talented stylist, or if her own attitudes were softening.

"It's different," Liz said, running her fingers through her hair, which now felt six inches longer.

Polly got to work trimming Liz's dead ends and shaping it a little around her face. When she was finished, Liz not only looked different, but felt five years younger.

"You look ready to catch a man," Polly exclaimed with another snort. "I love it!"

Polly ripped the gown off, sending the trimmed hair to the ground. Liz looked at the nail desk, but it seemed like Mandy had slipped out while she was being distracted by her hair. Fifty pounds lighter, Liz left the salon, tossing her straight hair over her shoulder.

She set off home, a new spring in her step. As she passed the market square, she noticed Simon packing up his stall. He looked up and stared at her for a moment, not seeming to recognise her. When the recognition kicked in, he quickly looked away.

Liz could not deny she felt a little disappointed. She almost wanted to explain her dinner date with Christopher, but she did not know what it would achieve, or why she cared so much that he should know it did not mean anything to her.

Nine

Paddy pulled eagerly on his lead as Liz walked towards Simon's farm, the hot sun beating down on her. The humidity had already turned her straight hair from the day before back to frizz. Deciding it would be better off her face, she paused to tie it at the base of her neck with the bobble around her wrist.

Relief surged through her when the farm came

into view on the horizon. Nancy had given her vague instructions, but Liz had wondered if she had been wandering aimlessly in the countryside for twenty minutes.

It looked bigger and more professional than the rundown farm she had imagined. There was a large, modern metal structure next to the old farmhouse, which she guessed was where the cows were milked for the cheese and ice cream. Liz walked past a giant tractor, unsure how her presence at the farm would be received.

She spotted a young man lifting a small hay bale, sweat dripping down his red face. He heaved it off the back of a truck before wiping away the sweat. She instantly recognised him as Frank's fired apprentice, Adam. Liz was going to leave the boy to his work, but Paddy had different ideas.

"*Paddy!*" Adam beamed as the dog ran towards the apprentice, his lead trailing behind him. "What are you doing up here?"

Adam bent over to stroke the dog before looking suspiciously up at Liz. She smiled at the young boy, hoping he was not about to tell her she was trespassing.

"You must be Liz," he said, holding out his hand. "I heard the new woman took over looking after Paddy. I didn't put two and two together when I saw you walking him at the pier the other day."

Liz smiled awkwardly, knowing he was bringing up their meeting at the pier before she had a chance to. It was a technique she had seen criminals apply in interviews when they wanted to control the narrative of a situation.

"I couldn't see him going to the shelter," Liz said, joining him in scratching behind the dog's floppy ears. "We've become quite the team."

"Frank would have wanted him to be looked after." Adam stood up and wiped his dirty hands on his faded jeans. "I think he's the only one the old bugger loved."

"Have you heard what happened to him?"

"The poisoning?" Adam asked, his young, chiselled features twisting, making him look older. "Word travels fast around here. I only found out this morning, but they're saying it was rat poison."

"Rat poison?" Liz echoed as she picked up Paddy's lead. "I never heard that part."

"I heard some woman talking about it on the

bus this morning," Adam said, shrugging defensively. "I think it was in today's paper."

"Are you working on the farm now?" she asked, looking around for a sign of Simon.

"It's only a couple of hours a week," Adam said as he wiped his face with the end of his t-shirt. "Simon's a good guy. It's weird to think I would have been without a job either way."

"Why's that?" Liz asked, deciding to play dumb. "Did you leave?"

"He fired me," Adam mumbled bitterly, his eyes narrowing on Liz. "Weren't you there? With that Turtle woman?"

"Was that you?" Liz replied. "My memory isn't what it was. Why did he fire you? Not catching enough fish?"

"I was good at that job, and he knew it," Adam said defensively. "He'd been acting weird for weeks, and then he suddenly flipped out one day out of the blue."

"That sounds odd."

"I think he found out I was seeing his daughter," Adam admitted. "We tried to keep it secret, but it's a small town. I can't help that I love her."

"Is that Mandy?" Liz asked, stroking behind Paddy's ears again. "The barmaid?"

"That's her," he said with a nod. "I'd seen her around a lot, but I didn't really speak to her until I started working for Frank. She was going through a messy divorce. I became a shoulder to cry on. We never meant for anything to happen, but it just did, you know? I don't even know why he'd be bothered. He was dating someone younger than him."

"Laura?" Liz asked. "I heard about that."

"What you probably *didn't* hear was that they split up a couple of days before he died," Adam continued, arching his brows at Liz. "Had a huge row in the Fish and Anchor. Mandy told me about it. Said Laura ran out in tears."

"They'd split up?" Liz echoed. "Why?"

"No idea," Adam said with a shrug. "I should really get on with this. I don't want it to look like I'm slacking. I can't afford to lose another job."

Liz nodded her understanding and turned around with Paddy. She almost considered leaving the farm immediately so she could go to her flat and think about everything Adam had told her, but she spotted Simon grooming a large golden horse outside a row of stables.

She was at the farm to try and diffuse the misunderstanding surrounding her non-date with '*Fishy Chris*', so that was exactly what she intended to do. With Paddy by her side, she set off across the yard, her heart stammering more with each step.

"*You were a detective,*" she whispered under her breath. "*Pull yourself together, woman.*"

She slipped into Simon's eye line, causing him to freeze. He gave her a similar uneasy look to the one he had given her when she had walked past the market the day before with her freshly straightened hair. She pushed forward her friendliest smile, hoping it would ease him.

"*L-Liz,*" he stuttered, his cheeks blushing. "I didn't expect to see you up here."

"I wanted some more of that delicious ice cream," she replied lightly. "It really is the best I've ever had."

"My ice cream?" Simon replied, scratching the side his head. "Didn't you have some on your date with Fishy Chris?"

"It wasn't a date," she replied sternly. "He asked if I wanted to go to dinner. I hadn't been to The Sea

Platter, so I accepted. Well, I didn't even accept. He just assumed I did."

"It's none of my business," Simon said with a shrug before continuing brushing the horse. "You can date who you want."

"It wasn't a date," she repeated again with a strained laugh. "I know you don't like him, but –"

"It's nothing to do with not liking him."

They stared at each other for a moment, both of them knowing what he meant, but neither of them wanting to admit it. Liz could not deny the chemistry she felt every time she was in the farmer's presence.

"Why don't I show you around?" Simon suggested. "I'll get this one back in her stable and give you the official tour."

"That sounds perfect," Liz said before letting out a relieved sigh. "Lead the way."

***

"I CAN'T BELIEVE EVERY ANIMAL ON THIS farm has a name," Liz said, sitting next to Simon on a large hay bale behind the stables. "How do you keep up?"

"This place is my whole life," he said, looking around with a contented smile. "It's going to be mine one day when my folks retire."

"Is that what you want?"

"It's all I want," he said bashfully. "I love it here."

"I can see why," Liz said, joining him in looking out at the sprawling fields. "It almost feels like this is the whole world."

"I suppose people think I'm a loser living up here with my parents still," Simon said after a lick of his ice cream. "Especially at my age."

"I don't think that," Liz reassured him. "It's sweet."

"I have my own little cottage behind the farm house," he said, nodding to the large house. "It's falling to pieces, but it's somewhere I can lock the door and get some sleep in peace." Simon paused to check the chunky watch on his wrist, instantly jumping up. "I didn't realise it was so late. The chickens were supposed to be fed half an hour ago. They'll be going crazy."

"I can't imagine they'd notice the time?" Liz

asked sceptically.

"They get fed on the dot every day," he said, holding his hand out for Liz to help her off the hay. "They're very particular. You can help, if you want?"

"Me?" Liz laughed awkwardly, accepting his hand. "I'm not really dressed for it."

"Sure you are," he said with a wink. "I'll lend you some wellies."

Simon grabbed a pair of muddy boots from the horse's tack room for her to cram her feet into. They were a little big, but they would do.

"This way," Simon exclaimed. "Keep up."

Feeling like her feet were not her own, Liz followed Simon with Paddy yanking on her arm. They rounded a corner, the large chicken enclosure coming into view. There had to be more than fifty chickens.

"Tie Paddy up there," Simon said, pointing at the fence.

Liz did as she was told, while Simon grabbed buckets of golden chicken feed from a tiny shed next to the enclosure. Simon passed a bucket to Liz with an amused look before unclipping the gate.

"Be careful," he cautioned with a dry smile.

"They might bite."

Liz laughed awkwardly, unsure if he was joking or not. Either way, she ignored her apprehension and followed him into the enclosure, reminding herself that she had dealt with the worst humanity had to offer; she could handle fifty chickens.

Once inside, the birds swarmed around their feet, proving Simon's point about them knowing when it was feeding time. She hoped they weren't so hungry that they were going to peck through her borrowed wellies.

"You just have to shuffle," Simon laughed as he demonstrated. "Scoop it out and toss it. They'll leave you alone when you feed them."

Liz nodded, dipping her hand into the grain. She watched Simon disperse the feed as he shuffled forward, so she copied his exact moves. Just when she thought she was getting the hang of it, she stepped back, her foot landing on one of the chickens. It startled her with a squawk, causing her to spin around. Before she realised what was happening, she landed on her backside, the bucket of grain flying from her hands, the feed sprinkling across her chest. The chickens swarmed around her, some of them jumping on her chest to treat her like an all you can eat buffet.

"*Leave her alone!*" Simon cried, clapping his hands together, causing the chickens to scatter. "Are you alright?"

"I think so," she mumbled, daring to open her eyes. "I'm not cut out for the farm life."

Simon chuckled as he held out a hand, which Liz gratefully accepted. Once back on her feet, she brushed the feed off her clothes, embarrassed she had made a simple task look so difficult.

"You're supposed to *scatter* the feed," Simon smiled warmly at her. "I've never seen anyone turn themselves into a platter before."

"I guess I can be the first," Liz said, rubbing her backside to wipe the dirt off. "It's nothing a change of clothes and a shower won't fix."

Simon chuckled softly as he stared deep into her eyes. He was so close that she could feel his breath on her. He reached towards her face, and for a second, she thought he was going to kiss her. She felt like her feet were suddenly glued to the ground.

"You've got some feed in your hair," he stated, plucking a piece of grain from her frizzy locks.

"That's better."

"Thank you," she said, embarrassed by her own thoughts. "I think we should leave the chickens to their food before they turn on me again."

Simon nodded his agreement before emptying out the rest of the buckets onto the ground. When he was done, they left the chickens to eat in peace. Liz felt more comfortable watching from the other side of the fence.

"Oh, here comes trouble," Simon whispered under his breath, nodding towards the farmhouse.

Liz looked up after untying Paddy. Ellie, Simon's little sister, was running across the yard, followed by a man and woman, who looked to be in their mid-sixties.

"Look, John, a guest!" the woman cried, winking at her husband. "Have you already put her to work, Simon?"

"Sandra, leave the boy alone," John cried, slapping his wife on the shoulder. "Feeding the chickens is hardly work."

"I made it look like hard work," Liz said, dusting down her front again. "You must be Simon's parents."

"Mum, Dad, this is Liz," Simon said, clearly uncomfortable by their sudden appearance.

"*Liz*!" Sandra exclaimed, taking her hand firmly. "So, *you're* the Liz we've heard so much about."

"You have?" Liz laughed nervously, feeling like a deer caught in the headlights, unsure if she had heard about her the same way the rest of Scarlet Cove had, or if she had heard something different through Simon. "All good things I hope. You've got a really nice place here."

"That's very sweet of you," John said, his eyes crinkling as he smiled, a grey moustache dancing on his top lip. "Isn't Liz sweet, Simon?"

"*Dad*," Simon said with a stern smile. "Why don't you get back inside?"

"I've just put the kettle on," Sandra said, glancing over her shoulder at the farmhouse, her hands tucking into her floral apron. "Would you like to stay for some tea, Liz?"

"I should probably set off home," Liz said awkwardly, hooking her thumb over her shoulder to the winding lane back to Scarlet Cove. "Paddy will be getting hungry."

"That's a shame," Sandra said, clearly assessing

the town's new arrival. "If you ever decide to visit again, our door is *always* open."

"And you're *always* welcome," John added, winking at his son. "C'mon, Ellie. Let's leave them to it."

Simon's parents hurried back to the farmhouse with Ellie skipping between them. They all looked back at Liz to wave before disappearing inside. When they were out of view, Simon let out a relieved sigh.

"I'm so sorry about them," he groaned with an unnatural laugh. "They're so embarrassing."

"They're sweet," Liz said. "It's okay. They clearly care about you."

Simon smiled his gratitude. It made Liz think about her own parents, and how much they would disapprove of Simon because of his upbringing and lifestyle. She almost wished her parents were more like Simon's.

They wandered past Adam, who was finishing unloading the hay, and to the edge of the farm. Simon hung back at the gate, leaning against the post.

"Like they said, you're always welcome up here,"

Simon said. "If you're ever passing, that is."

"I'll keep that in mind."

"See you later, Liz."

"Bye, Simon."

He nodded and saluted before turning and jogging back to the farmhouse. She watched him until he vanished from view, and then turned and set off down the winding lane. She only realised she had left without the tub of ice cream she had gone for when she was climbing the stairs to her flat.

Ten

Liz spent the next morning checking over everything in the shop, making sure she was ready for the grand opening. She was still waiting on a late order of canvases, and the printer had delayed fitting the new sign. Despite the setbacks, she was happy how things were coming together.

"What do you think?" she asked Paddy. He

looked up at her without a care in the world, panting with his tongue out. "That's what I thought."

She smiled and scratched the top of his head, and he nuzzled her hand appreciatively. Liz turned her back on him and got to work sorting out the display of pens on the counter, but she immediately turned back when she heard him whining near the back door at the end of the storeroom.

"Do you need to go?" she asked.

Paddy barked softly, ran in a circle, and looked up at her expectantly. Liz opened the door, instantly noticing the back gate was ajar. Before she had a chance to shut it, the dog bolted through the gap and out of sight.

"*Paddy!*" she shouted, running after him. "Come back!"

Paddy darted down the narrow alley and burst out onto the road at the end. After quickly locking the back door of her shop, she sprinted after him. As the wind rushed through her hair, she wondered if their relationship was more one sided than she had first thought.

He bolted across the road, narrowly missing a

car. Liz apologised with a wave of her hand before running in front of the car herself.

Paddy finally stopped in front of the Fish and Anchor. He cocked his leg against one of the flowerpots and relieved himself as he looked at Liz with a sheepish expression.

"You little rascal," she scolded him. "Don't do that again, okay? You gave me a fright."

Liz bent down and picked Paddy up when he was finished, her fingers wrapping around his collar in case he tried to dart off again. As she walked past the pub with Paddy in her arms, she looked down the alley and noticed Mandy leaning against the wall with a cigarette pressed between her lips. When Mandy noticed Liz, she quickly dropped the cigarette and stamped it out before blowing the smoke from her lungs.

"I quit ages ago," she said defensively. "It's been a long day. Is that my dad's dog?"

Liz walked down the dark alley towards the barmaid, taking the recognition of Paddy as an invitation to talk. After speaking with Adam at Simon's farm, she knew it would be good to hear Mandy's version of events, especially now that she knew Frank had been murdered.

"We could do with borrowing him," Mandy said, scratching the top of his head. "We keep getting rats in the yard. I'm supposed to be out here laying traps, but they don't seem to be making a difference."

"Have you tried rat poison?" Liz suggested, following Mandy into the tiny yard, which was filled with barrels and empty crates. "That's what I usually use."

"Shirley prefers we don't," Mandy admitted, glancing over her shoulder at the slightly open door. "But I use the stuff when she's off shift. We have a few boxes in the storeroom for emergencies. It's been a hot summer, so they keep coming back. I think they like the smell of the beer."

"Maybe this one could sniff them out," Liz said, letting Paddy down to the ground. "Do you have anything I could use as a lead? He's heavier than he looks."

Mandy dug in one of the empty crates and pulled out a strip of thin blue rope. Liz accepted it gratefully and threaded it through Paddy's collar.

"It's from the fish deliveries," Mandy explained.

"Fishy Chris wraps up the boxes in the stuff. I think he's paranoid someone is going to tamper with his stuff."

"Would someone do that?"

"Probably," Mandy said with a shrug. "He's not the nicest guy around here, is he?"

"Is that what your father said?"

Mandy narrowed her eyes at the mention of Frank. She wondered if she had spoken out of turn, but she was eager to find out more about their relationship from the source.

"He was ruthless," Mandy said. "Wanted to get rid of my dad from the start."

"Were you close?" Liz pushed.

"With my dad?" Mandy asked. "We used to be. I'm helping plan his funeral, and it's making me realise how little I actually knew him. Laura is sorting most of it out. If you want to know about my dad, you should ask her."

"I thought they'd split up?" Liz asked, remembering what Adam had told her. "Or so I heard."

"It doesn't matter now, does it?" Mandy said with a shrug, turning back to the door. "People split up all the time. It doesn't mean it's permanent. I should get back before Shirley sends out a search party."

Mandy strode back into the pub without saying another word. Liz lingered in the yard for a moment before heading back into the alley. Nancy had left this part of the pub off her tour. Liz wandered further down the alley, surprised when she came out into a beer garden at the back of the pub. It was full of men and women drinking pints and smoking cigarettes, their eyes glued on a game of football on a flat screen TV attached to the wall. One of the teams scored, causing half the crowd to roar, while the other booed.

From the beer garden, she had a perfect view into the pub. With Paddy by her side, Liz pushed through the crowd and into the building, which was just as busy inside. Thanks to the game of football, she went by unnoticed.

She considered ordering a glass of wine to take a little break from working on her shop. She got as far as the bar when she spotted Laura and Michael in the corner. Liz recognised it as the same corner Laura had been sitting in when she had been crying into her wine the day after Frank's death. The contrast between the two moments jumped out at Liz. Michael whispered something into Laura's ear, his fingers dancing up and down her arm. She tossed her head back and laughed before reaching for her wine glass.

Liz cast her mind back to their conversation in her shop the other day. Laura had still been grief-stricken then, but she seemed like a completely different woman now. Had what Adam said about Laura and Frank splitting up been true after all? And if it was true, had Laura rekindled her relationship with her estranged husband? Before Liz could observe anymore, the couple stood up and walked through to the beer garden. She bobbed her head, but they looked too lost in their own world to notice her.

Liz knew grief was not a straight line. After Lewis' death, she would spend days crying in the shower, and others laughing manically in a wine bar with people she barely knew. Michael was likely to be a familiar comfort to Laura, and Liz could not begrudge her a shred of happiness in the bleakness that had followed since finding his body.

Deciding against taking a break in a pub full of football fans, Liz headed through the front door. She paused on the doorstep and inhaled the sea air, glad of the peace and quiet. Her momentary bubble of peace popped when a familiar voice floated down the street towards her. Liz turned to see Christopher and his sister, Katelyn, walking arm in arm towards her. When they saw her, they had two very different reactions.

"Good afternoon, Elizabeth," Christopher beamed, seeming to have forgotten all about her awkwardly dodging his kiss after their non-date. "Beautiful day, wouldn't you say?"

"It is," she said shortly. "I'm still not used to this sea breeze. Cools everything down when you need it the most."

Christopher nodded his agreement, but Katelyn's glaze remained blank and steely. Liz was not keen to relive her first meeting with Katelyn anytime soon. She almost wished she could have made as quick an escape as Paddy had.

"Nice to see you again, Elizabeth." Katelyn's strained smile was obvious. "What a lovely dog you have there."

"You two have already met?" Christopher asked, looking at both of the women. "You didn't mention it, Katelyn."

"Briefly," Liz said bluntly.

"Elizabeth was kind enough to bring some of her work in, and it pained me to not be able to show it in our gallery," Katelyn said, her strained smile growing. "We just don't have the space."

Liz narrowed her eyes on the woman, her heart squirming in her chest. Just from the dopey look on Christopher's face, Liz doubted he would believe her if she said anything to contradict his sister's version of events. Knowing it was not worth it, Liz decided it would be better to play Katelyn at her own game.

"You must let me know if any spaces become available," Liz said airily. "You did, after all, love my work."

Katelyn's smile faltered, but she maintained her composure, simply nodding stiffly. When Paddy pulled on the makeshift lead, Liz was grateful for the excuse to leave.

"I'll see you around," Liz said, making sure to look them both in the eyes while she smiled her goodbyes. "I think Paddy would like to continue his walk."

Eager not to let either of the uptight siblings have the last word, Liz hurried around them, setting off down the winding street, the bright sun shining gloriously down on her. Her bubble of peace almost re-formed around her, until she heard footsteps hurrying after her.

"Are you heading down to the harbour?" Christopher called as he caught up with her. "I'll walk with you."

Liz opened her mouth to object until she realised it had not been a question. Just like their date, Christopher had assumed her acceptance of his company.

"Settling in?" he asked as they turned onto one of Scarlet Cove's many twisting backstreets.

"As much as a city person can in a small town," Liz said. "I think I was wrong to assume coastal life would be a lot slower. I don't think I've ever been busier."

"Small town life is certainly different." Christopher replied thoughtfully. "The city is much better for business, but I've been here so long, I don't think I'd want to leave."

"You seem to be doing well here," Liz said.

"Oh, I am, but there is always space for growth. I just don't think now would be the time. I was hoping to bump into you."

"You were?" Liz mumbled, already knowing what was coming next. "Why's that?"

"I thoroughly enjoyed our date the other night," Christopher said, the nerves obvious in his voice. "I think you did too, so I would love to arrange a second one."

Liz wondered if she had given off any signals that she had enjoyed their non-date, or if it was wishful thinking on Christopher's part.

"It wasn't really a date, was it?" she reminded him. "I don't really think now is the right time for me, Christopher. I'm going to be really busy getting things ready for the shop opening."

Christopher nodded his understanding. To Liz's surprise, he did not push the subject, and they walked in silence until they reached his office at the harbour.

"Can I at least invite you in for some coffee or tea?" he asked his teeth sparkling as he smiled. "As friends?"

Liz looked through the window of his office and tried to think of a polite way to decline. She opened her mouth to speak, stopping when something caught her eye on one of Christopher's crowded shelves. She squinted to make sure she was not mistaken. Even with her waning eyesight, she could read the large label on the metal tin easily; rat poison.

"Coffee would be lovely," she said, pushing forward a smile. "I've been mainly drinking tea recently, so it would make a nice change."

Liz sat down in the chair in front of Christopher's desk. She held Paddy's lead tight by her side as she assessed the poison label from closer up. Christopher smiled over his shoulder as he put a pod into his coffee machine. She smiled back, looking away from the poison until he turned back to the cups.

Liz was eager to inspect the tin, but she knew she could not do it without Christopher questioning her. Deciding it would be better to play along like she had done with Katelyn, Liz relaxed into her chair and waited for Christopher to finish making the coffee.

"Rat poison?" Liz asked as he set the drink in front of her and sat on the other side of the desk. "Mandy said they're running havoc at the pub too. I hope they stay away from my shop."

"I think they like the sea air," he replied lightly as he blew on the surface of his coffee. "They're quite the nuisance. I bought this stuff online. It's the strongest you can legally buy. I can order you some if you like? The tiniest bit is enough to kill any rat, even the bigger ones."

"Maybe I should invest in some," she said airily, wondering if she was looking at the murder weapon. "I'll wait until I actually see some at the shop. I don't want Paddy coming across it."

"Good idea," he said after a sip of his coffee. "It is highly lethal to animals."

"Humans too?"

"I suppose it is," he said with a shrug. "Don't go eating any, right?"

Christopher laughed, his teeth dazzling her from across the table. Liz attempted to join in, but she felt too uneasy. Did Christopher know she knew how Frank had died? Was he bragging? Liz wanted to ask him so many questions but had no clue where to start. Without her detective's badge, she felt powerless.

"About that date," Liz said, resting her untouched cup on the desk. "Why don't you come to my place tomorrow night? I'll cook."

"You cook?"

"Sure," she lied. "Lots of things."

"What changed your mind?"

"Oh, I don't know," Liz said, scrambling for any reason other than the truth. "It would be nice to cook for someone in my new kitchen."

"That sounds perfect," he said. "I'll see you tomorrow, Elizabeth."

Liz left Christopher to get on with his work without even having taken a sip of her coffee. With Paddy by her side, she walked back towards her shop, wondering if she had just made a stupid mistake. It was not just a case of leading Christopher on; she could not cook even if her life depended on it. Could Christopher really have murdered Frank, or was it just a coincidence that he also had rat poison? How many other people in the town had access to poison?

Pushing the thoughts to the back of her mind,

Liz turned her attention to what she was going to cook for Christopher. Could she buy a takeaway meal and hope he did not notice? After slurping oysters in The Sea Platter, she was not sure a Chinese takeaway and a bottle of wine from the corner shop would go down too well. Even if it was not a real date, she wanted him to be relaxed enough so she could covertly interview him.

Liz walked past the pub, and cast an eye down the alley beside it, half expecting to see Mandy having another sly cigarette while the football match played inside. Instead, she saw something far more unsettling.

With Paddy by her side, Liz walked carefully down the alley, her eyes trained on a hand poking out of the yard's door, a mousetrap on the end of the fingers. Just from the tightness of the knuckles, Liz suspected the worst.

Pushing on the back door, she let out a gasp when she saw the scene in front of her. Paddy barked loudly, the lead slipping out of her hand. He ran into the yard, pushing the door wide open, immediately resting by the body's side.

"It's too late, boy," she gulped, aware of the

shakiness in her voice. "He's dead."

Liz stared down into the eyes of Adam, as he stared lifelessly back at her in a pool of his own blood, a green glass bottle lodged in his throat. The pub's back door opened and Mandy slipped out with a packet of cigarettes clenched in her fist. Mandy noticed Liz, and then she spotted her dead boyfriend on the ground between them. She let out a blood-curdling scream, which Liz recognised all too well.

Eleven

Liz found herself outside Driftwood Café late the next morning, waiting for Nancy. For the first time since arriving in Scarlet Cove, clouds blocked the sun, and the sea breeze felt more like an icy chill than anything soothing. Liz's red hair broke free of her ears and fluttered across her face, making her wish she had tied it back. She tucked it back and pulled her cardigan across her chest, glad when she saw Nancy scurrying down the street towards her in a bright yellow skirt and a pink shirt.

"Sorry I'm late!" Nancy cried. "There was a mix-up at the gallery. Our gift shop stock got mixed up with that of a kids' toyshop, and I don't think Katelyn would have been very happy to see us selling rattles and jigsaws."

"It's okay," Liz replied, forcing back a yawn. "I didn't get much sleep last night."

"I'm not surprised," Nancy said, rubbing Liz's arm. "Seeing two dead bodies in the space of a week can't be the best thing. Stuff like this *never* happens here."

"That's what the police kept saying last night. The fact I used to be a detective didn't seem to mean anything to them. They were questioning me until midnight."

"Do they think you have something to do with it?" Nancy asked, clutching her mouth. "That's *awful*!"

"Well, I did find both bodies. I'd suspect me too."

Leaving the icy breeze, they walked into the small café. Cheerful cornflower blue walls and matching chairs made a smart contrast with black and white square tiles, the tables covered in red and white gingham tablecloths. Much to Liz's relief, the café was quiet. She did not doubt news of her finding Adam's body had spread like wildfire, but she was not in the mood to answer more questions.

The café's elderly owner, Violet Lloyd, came over when they sat at a table near the window. Her greying hair was pulled back into a netted bun, and her face, while lined, still had a youthful quality to it.

"What can I get you ladies?" she asked with a smile, licking a pencil and flipping to a new page in her notepad. "The cheese and onion pie is exceptionally delicious today."

"Can I have an ice cream float?" Nancy asked after glancing over the menu. "Cheese and onion pie sounds good to me."

"Me too," Liz said, not in the mood to look over the unfamiliar menu. "I'll have the same."

Violet scurried away and into the kitchen behind the counter. Nancy smiled sympathetically across the table at Liz, seeming to notice her low mood. When Nancy had called that morning insisting to meet for lunch, Liz had been touched that she had met someone who cared so much about her, even if she had wanted to spend the day under the covers in the solace of her flat.

"If you don't want to talk about it, you don't have to," Nancy said, obviously intrigued. "We can talk about the weather or Simon?"

"You're itching to ask me everything, aren't you?"

"Folks *have* been gossiping," Nancy said apologetically. "I just want to know the facts straight from the detective's mouth."

"*Retired* detective."

Violet hurried over with their ice cream floats on a tray. She quickly put them on the table and hurried away again.

"It was definitely foul play," Liz said, knowing the subject was unavoidable. "He had a broken bottle sticking out of his throat. He didn't fall into it."

Nancy's eyes opened wide as she slurped on her straw.

"I thought people were exaggerating," Nancy gasped. "A *bottle*?"

"It wasn't a nice sight," Liz replied before sipping her drink.

"Who would want to do that to Adam?" Nancy wondered aloud, wiping ice cream from her lips. "He was just a kid. He wouldn't harm a fly."

"It's obvious, isn't it?" Liz mumbled through a mouthful of ice cream. "Whoever killed Frank killed Adam too. I had suspected Adam might have been the one to poison the man who fired him, but apparently not."

"Why would they want to kill Adam too?"

"Maybe he knew something that someone didn't want him to tell anyone about?" Liz suggested after another sip. "Or, he figured out the truth, which if he did, means he was a better detective than I am."

"Don't you have suspects?" Nancy urged, shuffling forward on her chair. "You *must* have it figured out by now."

"What part of *retired* means nothing around here?" Liz asked with a stilted laugh. "Of course I have suspects, but this isn't my case. I can't start interviewing people to find out what I want to know."

"But you *have* been asking questions, right?"

"Out of habit, more than anything," Liz admitted. "So far, I've narrowed my list down to a handful of people. I couldn't really sleep last night, so I had time to think about it."

"Who?" Nancy asked excitedly. "Tell me."

Liz noticed Violet edging across the café with their food, so she decided to wait. She turned and looked out of the window. She spotted Mandy walking past the market square, presumably on her way from the pub. She looked well put together considering her boyfriend and father had died in the same week.

"Is Mandy on your list?" Nancy asked, following Liz's gaze. "Look at her walking around as if nothing has happened. I couldn't face getting out of bed if Dad and Jack died. It doesn't even bear thinking about."

Violet put their food in front of them before hurrying back behind the counter. Liz looked at the cheese and onion pie with her knife and fork in hand, unsure if she was even hungry.

"What would her motive be?" Liz asked. "What does she get from killing them both?"

"A motive? This is *so* exciting. You sound like

you're back on the job. Aren't the police looking into it?"

"Of course," Liz said with a nod as she cut into the crust. "They took statements from everyone at the pub last night. They gave me the impression they don't deal with murder a lot."

"Well, they don't," Nancy said. "It's only Scarlet Cove. Nothing ever happens here."

"Everyone thought Frank's death was an accident," Liz countered. "I always sensed something else, and I was right. Now that Adam is dead too, it's hard to deny there's definitely something happening here, Scarlet Cove, or not."

"Just don't go getting yourself killed," Nancy urged. "I've become pretty attached to you."

They both tucked into their pies, and as Liz suspected, it was delicious. She wondered if Simon's cheese was involved in the flavour.

"It would seem Laura and Michael are back together," Liz said after she swallowed a mouthful of the pie. "They looked rather close at the pub yesterday before —"

"Laura and Michael?" Nancy jumped in. "Back together? I don't think so. That's just how they are.

They stayed friends after she left him for Frank. Maybe it's a little strange, but they've known each other for so long, but it's better than constantly arguing. I couldn't imagine breaking up with Jack and having to see him every day. I suppose it would be easier to be civil."

"They looked *more* than civil," Liz added after another mouthful. "They looked like –"

Before Liz could finish her sentence, Simon walked into the café carrying a crate, his face pale, and his eyes red. He headed into the kitchen with Violet.

"What's that look?" Nancy asked with a sly smile. "You're blushing."

"No, I'm not," Liz fired back, her cheeks hot. "There is no look."

"I heard about your little chicken feeding date."

"Why does everyone in this town think it's a date every time a man and woman spend more than ten minutes together?"

"Because it usually is."

Liz twirled her fork around in the pie mixture. She had to admit her interaction with Simon at the farm had felt more like a date than anything she had experienced with Christopher, which made her feel even guiltier for her planned date with Christopher that evening. She had almost cancelled that morning, but her need to question Christopher had prevented her.

Simon walked out of the kitchen with the empty crate, his eyes meeting Liz's. His smile twisted like a knife in her stomach, but she tried her best to smile back.

"How are you doing, Simon?" Nancy asked. "I heard Adam was working for you."

"I'm doing okay," he said with a shrug. "Adam didn't deserve this. He was a good lad. I just don't know why anyone would do that to him."

"They will be caught," Liz assured him. "It's almost impossible to hide when you've killed twice."

Simon nodded, seeming soothed by her reassurance. She knew she was in no position to speak on behalf of the police, but if she had been the detective in charge of the case, she was sure she would have wrapped things up soon after Frank's death.

"The CCTV was wiped at the pub," Simon said as he scratched the side of his head. "That's what

Shirley said, at least. It could be anyone. I heard it was busy yesterday with the football."

"Well, whoever it was, they're going to great lengths to cover their tracks," Liz said, trying to avoid Nancy's '*I told you so*' look. "They can't hide forever."

"I hope not," he said with a forced smile. "I'll see you girls later. I have to get back to the farm."

Liz nodded, ignoring the foreign urge she had inside to hug Simon.

"I didn't realise they were that close," Liz remarked, pushing her half-finished pie away. "He seems so upset."

"He's a sensitive guy," Nancy replied, pulling Liz's leftovers towards her after finishing her own. "Adam used to help him out now and then when he wasn't fishing. You know what guys are like. They bond over burping and football in five seconds if you leave them in a room together. Are you going to finish this?"

Liz shook her head. She slurped her drink, the ice cream having completely melted into the fizzy pop.

"Whoever wiped the CCTV must have known

what they were doing," Liz thought aloud. "It knocks one person off my list of suspects."

"It's not Mandy, is it?" Nancy asked as she stared at Liz's pie. "She was there, and she would know how to wipe the CCTV. The woman *works* there."

"She's probably the police's prime suspect," Liz said. "And it's Christopher that I've wiped off. I just realised I was with him at the harbour when it happened. Even if he had somehow killed Adam in the time it took for me to walk from the yard and into the pub, he wouldn't have had time to wipe the CCTV, run around, meet his sister and then bump into me."

"Christopher was a suspect?" Nancy asked. "Why?"

"Because he wanted to fire Frank, and he had rat poison in his office." Liz paused and slurped up the last of her drink. "And I'm not saying Mandy *didn't* do it, but I still can't pin a motive to her."

"You're the detective," Nancy said with a shrug. "You'll figure it out. I have faith in you."

Liz smiled at her friend before motioning to Violet to send the bill over. Miles used to say similar things to her back in Manchester. Even if she had no clue where to start or what evidence to focus on first, his confidence in her skills had always given her the boost she had needed.

After splitting the bill, they walked out into the chilly air. Michael was sitting on a bench on the edge of the empty market square, bundled up in a scarf and jacket.

"Poor guy," Nancy said as she pulled her handbag over her shoulder. "Maybe it would be better if Laura finally cut ties. I think he's holding out that she'll take him back. I should get back to the gallery. The dragon lady will start spitting flames if I'm even two seconds late."

Nancy hugged Liz, leaving her to walk back to her flat alone. When she was back inside, she sat on the couch with Paddy by her feet. She pulled out her phone and scrolled to Miles' name. She almost called him but stopped herself. She did not want to worry him, nor did she want to admit he had been right about small town life being even more hectic than city life. Tossing her phone onto the coffee table, she walked into the kitchen and poured herself a large glass of wine, not caring that it was the middle of the afternoon.

Sitting at the kitchen table with her wine, she tried to piece the dots together. The only person she could connect both Frank and Adam to was Mandy. Was Nancy right? Could Mandy have really killed her father and boyfriend? Liz took a deep sip of her wine, sure she was missing something right under her nose.

Twelve

The buzzer went off, almost on cue. Liz looked down at the mess she had made in her kitchen while attempting to prepare spaghetti Bolognese, the easiest meal she could think to make.

"Just a second," she called as she ripped her apron off, before bending over and picking up the fallen mushrooms and onion.

After giving the bubbling red mixture one last

stir, she ran across her flat, almost tripping over Paddy, who was sprawled across the floor in front of the flickering muted television. Liz unlocked the front door with a press of a button. She tossed her hair over her shoulder, wiped her sauce-covered hands on the back of her black jeans, opened the door, and applied her friendliest smile.

"Hi," she said breathlessly when Christopher reached the top of the stairs. "Right on time."

"Hello, Elizabeth," Christopher said, offering a bottle of wine. "I hope you don't mind, but I brought my own bottle. I have particular tastes. You look lovely, as always."

"Thanks," she mumbled, wondering if he could see where the sauce had spit all over her shirt. "This looks like good wine. I heard if a bottle of wine has a map on the back, it's the good stuff."

Christopher blinked vacantly as she closed the door behind him. She laughed nervously, unsure of why she was acting so strangely. Reminding herself it was not a real date, she took the wine through to the kitchen.

"I like what you've done with the place," Christopher said as he looked around the bare flat.

"It's very minimal. Did you paint this?"

He paused and nodded at the painting of the sunset hanging over the fireplace.

"I painted it looking out of that window," Liz said. "Do you like it?"

Christopher assessed the picture for a moment, tilting his head as he tapped his finger against his chin.

"I dare say I do," he said. "It's different."

"Your sister hated it."

"She did?" Christopher asked, arching a brow. "Well, I suppose she *is* the expert."

Liz grabbed two glasses from the cupboard and wondered what qualified Katelyn to be the authoritative voice on art. She cracked open the expensive wine and filled the glasses to the top.

"Generous measure," Christopher commented when Liz joined him in staring at the painting. "When is your grand opening? I hope I'm invited."

"Everyone is invited," she said vaguely. "Next Saturday, I hope. I haven't decided a date yet. I'm still waiting on some stock arriving."

Christopher nodded before sipping his wine. Liz copied him, taking an even bigger gulp. She could sense the awkward tension in the air, which she had not been expecting. For her, it was an opportunity to question Christopher properly, but for him, he was on a date. Had she used the word '*date*' when inviting him to dinner? She could not remember, so she took another gulp of wine.

"Can you smell burning?" he asked, wrinkling his nose and turning to the kitchen.

"*Bloody hell!*" she cried. "*The Bolognese!*"

Liz ran through to the kitchen and sighed when she saw her sauce bubbling over. It had spat red liquid all over her kitchen. She quickly turned down the heat and attempted to stir it, but it had completely stuck to the bottom of the pan.

"It's *ruined*," she groaned as she scraped at the burnt sauce. "This is why I don't cook."

She turned to Christopher, expecting him to look disappointed, but he looked amused at her feeble attempt to cook dinner for them.

"It's not funny," she snapped, frowning as she tossed the wooden spoon onto the messy chopping board. "The recipe I was following said this was easy."

"It *is* easy," Christopher said. "If not a little

common."

He set his wine glass next to hers before taking off his jacket. After yanking off his tie, he rolled up his sleeves and opened her fridge.

"What are you doing?" she asked as she poured the ruined sauce into the bin. "You're not going to find a lobster or a pot of caviar in there."

"Do you like omelettes?" he asked, pulling out a tray of eggs. "You have everything to make one."

"I do?" she replied, joining him in looking at her almost bare fridge. "I can't say I've ever made one."

"Omelettes it is," Christopher said, grabbing the milk and putting it next to the eggs on the counter. "Stand back. I've got this."

Liz did as she was told and stepped back. She clung to her wine glass as she watched Christopher clear away her mess. He quickly scrubbed the frying pan clean, dried it with a towel, and put it on the hob. After looking in her almost empty cupboards, he found a glass mixing bowl and began cracking the eggs. After half a dozen, he added a splash of milk, a dash of salt and pepper, and whisked with a fork.

"The trick is not to let the pan get too hot," he said as he clicked on the gas hob. "That's how things burn."

"I know *that* much."

Christopher smiled over his shoulder as he poured the egg mixture into the pan. For the first time since meeting him, he almost seemed like a real human being.

"Where did you learn to cook?" Liz asked as she watched. "I always wondered if I should take lessons, but I never seemed to have time."

"It's embarrassing."

"I won't judge," Liz coaxed. "I promise."

"One of my only friends growing up was the cook," Christopher mumbled, glancing at Liz over his shoulder. "He was called Ray Murphy. I'd get bored in that big empty house, so I'd sit and watch him cook. He'd let me help sometimes. He died a long time ago, but he passed on most of his knowledge to me. I actually enjoy cooking for people, not that I ever have anyone to cook for. The omelette is nearly done, so why don't you take a seat in the front?"

"You want us to eat on our knees in front of the TV?" Liz asked, glancing at the table she had set, which was now dotted with her failed sauce.

"I'm not completely uptight," he said, flashing her another toothy grin. "It's how I eat most nights when I'm alone."

Leaving him to dish up, Liz sat on the couch and un-muted the television. It was on a soap opera she had never had time to watch back in Manchester, but had somehow been sucked into since moving to Scarlet Cove. She flicked through the channels, landing on the local news. A picture of Adam flashed up on the screen next to one of Frank. She quickly flicked to the next channel, not wanting to give away her motive too soon.

Liz flicked to a quiz show as Christopher walked in with two plates, half of the large omelette on each.

"They'd be better if I'd had some ham and peppers to throw in," he said as he sat next to her on the couch after passing her a plate. "But you can't go wrong with a basic omelette."

Liz tucked into the delicious omelette, surprised he had whipped it up from the basic rations in her fridge. She had considered falling back on two of the microwave meals in her freezer if things had gone wrong, but she was almost embarrassed by the mountain of frozen food she had in comparison to fresh.

"This is really good," she said through a mouthful. "You saved the day."

"It's nothing," he said. "I've never been a huge fan of spaghetti anyway."

They watched the quiz as they finished their omelettes. Christopher seemed to know the answers to all of the questions based around anything slightly intellectual, but did not have a clue when it came to the pop culture based questions, which Liz was slightly better at answering.

"Christopher, can I ask you something?" she asked when they put their plates on the coffee table as the advertisements played during the break.

"Of course," Christopher replied, turning to face her with a hopeful smile. "Ask me anything."

"It's about Frank and Adam."

"Oh," he mumbled, his expression dropping. "Go ahead."

Liz inhaled deeply, unsure of where to start. She decided against admitting that she had thought Christopher could have possibly been involved.

"Do you have any idea who could have killed them?" Liz asked tactfully. "You worked with both of them, so I thought you might have some insight that I'm missing."

"You sound like the police," he said with a sad smile, as though he had just realised the true nature of their date. "They interviewed me this afternoon. I told them that I was with you when Adam was found dead, which seemed to settle them."

"I told them that last night," Liz said. "I didn't want you getting into trouble."

"Why would I?"

"No reason," she replied quickly, her mind turning to the rat poison in his office. "Do you have any thoughts about any of this?"

"I've been thinking about it a little too," Christopher admitted. "I liked Adam more than Frank, that's for sure. I almost offered the kid a job myself, but I didn't think he was experienced enough to take over Frank's boat. I heard he landed on his feet at the farm, so I didn't feel too bad."

"You heard about how Frank died, right?" Liz asked before sipping her wine. "It was rat poison, no doubt in his hip flask. The police wouldn't confirm it last night, but I could tell it was true when I asked them. They were too outraged that I'd heard for it to be a lie."

"How did you hear?"

"Gossip," she said. "It has its perks living somewhere so small. Nothing seems to stay secret."

"That's true," Christopher replied with a nod. "Katelyn heard about our date at the restaurant before I had a chance to tell her. I suppose someone called her as soon as they saw us."

Liz gulped down more wine, not wanting to remind him again that it had not been a date.

"Back to the rat poison," she said, eager to know more. "You have a huge tub of the stuff in your office."

"*Had*," he said. "The police took it this afternoon after I mentioned it. I thought that was a peculiar move."

"Do you think it was the same poison that killed Frank?" Liz asked, knowing there was more than one tub of poison in the town.

"I didn't really use the stuff that often," Christopher admitted. "I did put some down the morning after Frank's death. The rodents had been chewing through the nets again, and they're quite expensive to replace. I did notice there was a lot less than I remembered, but I didn't think anything of it. The morning Frank died, I was out of the office all day at a meeting over in Cornwall. When I came back, I came and talked to you while you were painting, and well – you know the rest."

"So, someone broke into your office and stole some?" Liz suggested. "But how did they get it into his hip flask? I heard he didn't let the thing out of his sight."

Christopher's eyes widened, and he clasped his hand over his mouth.

"I took it off him the day before he was found, in the pub," Christopher said through his fingers. "I heard from the other fishers that he was blind drunk when he pulled into the harbour, so I marched into the Fish and Anchor and demanded that he hand it over, and told him he could have it back when he stopped drinking at work."

"Was the pub full?"

"*Everyone* was there," he said with a nod.

"Who's everyone?"

"You know," Christopher mumbled with a shrug. "The usual faces."

"Do you lock your office door?" Liz asked, her

voice shaking.

"Not always. I leave it open because the guys leave their keys in there. I always lock it overnight, but –"

"Whoever poisoned Frank probably saw what happened at the pub and snuck in the next morning to spike his hip flask with the rat poison, knowing that Frank would likely just take it back."

"Does that mean it's my fault?" Christopher asked, appearing remorseful about his head fisher's death for the first time. "I feel so guilty."

"Whoever killed Frank would have done it anyway, I suspect," Liz assured him, resting a hand on his shoulder. "I just think you gave them their window of opportunity. If it wasn't the rat poison, it would have been a stabbing, or something else."

"But who?"

"I don't know," Liz replied, pulling her hand back and sinking into the couch. "That's what I'm struggling with. Nancy thinks it's Mandy, but I can't think of a motive."

"She was there a couple of days before," Christopher said, tapping his finger on his chin. "I remember because I rarely saw her down there. She was demanding money from him, but he wasn't entertaining her. She stormed off, telling him he would regret it."

"Money for what?"

"Probably to get her hair done," Christopher suggested with a shrug. "I heard her husband was quite wealthy, but she walked away with nothing in the divorce."

Liz thought about what he had said for a minute. It was a motive, especially if she had threatened him, but why Adam too? Had he figured out what Mandy had done, and she had killed him to cover her tracks?

"This isn't a date, is it?" Christopher asked suddenly. "This isn't a date any more than the restaurant was a date."

Liz looked down into her wine, unable to look the man in the eyes.

"I'm sorry," she said feebly. "It's the detective in me. She takes over sometimes."

"It's okay," he said, standing up and putting his glass on the table next to the plates. "I got to have dinner twice with the most beautiful woman in Scarlet Cove."

Liz blushed and gulped down more of the wine. She was sure Christopher was trying to make her feel better for being such an awful person, but it just made her feel worse.

"I'll show you to the door," she said awkwardly. "I think we'd be better suited as friends. I do like you, Christopher."

"Thank you," he said with a genuine smile. "I can't remember the last time I heard that, if ever."

Liz walked him to the door, not wanting to mention that more people would like him if he stopped so blatantly looking down his nose at everyone else in Scarlet Cove. Considering his shallow and lonely upbringing, she could hardly blame the man for his stunted social skills.

"I had a lovely evening regardless," Christopher said as he unrolled his sleeves and pulled on his jacket. "Thank you for the food."

"I should thank you. We'd have been eating burnt Bolognese otherwise."

"That is true," he chuckled. "You can keep the rest of the wine. You seemed to enjoy it."

Liz glanced back at her almost empty glass, which was rather embarrassing next to his almost untouched brimming glass.

After opening the door, Christopher shook her hand instead of attempting to kiss her again. He turned back at the bottom of the stairs before heading out into the street. She waved at him, and he waved back, his sad smile saying it all.

"You're a terrible person," Liz mumbled to herself after closing the door. "Do you agree, Paddy?"

The dog looked up from his spot by the window, but he was not interested in what she had to say. He curled back up and went straight back to sleep.

Liz took the plates and glasses back into the kitchen. When she was in there, she grabbed the bottle of wine and turned it over. It did, indeed, have a map pointing out which region of Italy it was from. Out of curiosity, Liz searched for the price online, instantly regretting it when she saw it cost almost as much as her shop's rent for a week.

After pouring Christopher's leftover wine into her own glass and putting the bottle in the fridge, she walked back into the sitting room and grabbed a large, blank canvas. She rested it against her easel next to Paddy before balancing her glass on the windowsill. With a paintbrush and a little black paint, she wrote '*Frank Troughton*' in the centre and everything she knew around his name. When she was done, she stepped back and looked at her investigation board, which looked like a rudimentary version of the ones she used to make back at the station.

"What am I missing, Paddy?" she asked her companion, who looked up at her, his expression as perplexed as she felt. "That's what I thought."

Thirteen

Liz slipped into her only black dress, still unsure about whether attending Frank's funeral was the right decision. She had not officially been invited by his family, but she knew that was not how funerals worked. The detective in her knew the high emotions of the day might cause someone to slip up, and if they did, she wanted to be there to witness it.

As she forced pins into the frizzy bun she had

made at the back of her head, she walked through to the sitting room and stared at the canvas hanging above her fireplace. She was still none the wiser, despite the investigation board having been on her living room wall for the last four days. She had considered taking a picture to send to Miles, if only to get his opinion. The only thing that had stopped her was how insistent she had been that Scarlet Cove would be a fresh start for her, and it had only taken her just over a week to revert back to what she knew.

She stuffed her feet into her black kitten heels, grabbed her only black handbag, and popped her phone and keys inside, along with a packet of tissues that she had bought from the corner shop, just in case anyone needed one. She was not the type of person to show emotion at funerals, especially not when all eyes were on her. She had somehow managed to hold it together through Lewis' funeral, if only to convince her family and friends they did not need to keep ringing her and asking how she was.

She walked towards the door, ready to leave, but stopped when she noticed Paddy by the door. He whimpered and looked up at her, his wide eyes showing some recognition of what day it was.

"I can't take you, boy," she apologised, scratching behind his ears. "I don't think dogs are allowed in churches."

Paddy jumped up and ran in a circle. Liz sighed and grabbed his lead from the hooks on the wall.

"You *were* his dog," she mumbled to herself. "If anyone says anything, we'll leave. Deal?"

Liz walked across town with Paddy, noticing an unusual silence in the streets. It seemed even the seagulls above had decided to forego their shrill squawking for one day.

St. Andrew's Church sat on a winding corner on a steep hill Liz had yet to explore. She had not known if the funeral would be well attended or not, but she could see that most of Scarlet Cove were waiting for the funeral cars to arrive. Pulling Paddy closer, Liz approached the church cautiously, yanking down her dress's tight skirt. When her eyes met with Nancy's, she was relieved to see a familiar face.

"Liz!" Nancy called as loudly as she dared. "Over here. Oh, you've brought Paddy. Frank would have wanted him here."

A couple of people looked down at the dog as Liz made her way through the thick crowd, but she was glad when none of them seemed too bothered or outraged by his presence.

"This is my dad, Tim," Nancy said, pushing forward a balding man in his late-fifties. "He runs the lighthouse. Dad, this is the Liz I've been telling you about."

"How do you do," the man grunted. "Nice to put a name to a face."

"Me too," Liz said with a chuckle. "Tim Turtle. Funny name."

Nancy and Tim looked at each other, neither of them seeming to find it funny. Liz coughed and looked down at Paddy.

As though to save her, three funeral cars pulled up outside the church on the steep lane. The first was the hearse with the coffin in the back, which was suspiciously absent of any flowers. Mandy got out of the second black car, and Laura got out of the third. Liz wondered if it was entirely necessary for the women to take separate cars, but she did not vocalise her question.

Frank's fellow fishermen carried the coffin on

their shoulders through the sombre crowd, all of them in their usual fishing attire. One man stuck out in a sharp suit, and Liz was surprised to see it was Christopher. He spotted her and smiled before frowning down at the dog.

Mandy and Laura followed the coffin into the church, neither of them crying, but Laura looking more the part than Mandy, who was plastered in too much makeup as usual.

Liz hung back with Nancy and Tim, and they were the last to make their way into the church. They took seats in the last pew, between Violet from the café and Polly from the hairdressers. Both women smiled their recognition of Liz and Nancy.

With Paddy at her feet, Liz faced the front of the church, more concerned with Mandy and Laura than the priest reading blankly from the Bible. There were a few stifled sniffles and sobs here and there, but the church remained unusually silent for such a good turnout. Liz had been to her fair share of funerals thanks to her job. She knew the well-attended funerals were usually because the deceased had been popular. In Scarlet Cove, it seemed like most of the people were there for similar reasons to herself; to be nosey. It almost made her feel guilty, but she knew she was likely to be the only person in the sea of faces who wanted to catch the murderer before another body turned up.

When the priest finished with his reading, Liz's ears pricked up when she heard him announce that Frank's partner, Laura, was going to perform Frank's eulogy. Laura stepped up to the lectern, the piece of paper trembling in her hands. She cleared her throat before looking around the packed church.

"Frank was a great man," she started, her voice unsure as she read aloud from the paper. "I know many people here didn't know him as well as they would have wanted to, and to me, that's a shame." She paused and sighed before folding up the paper and tucking it into her pocket. "He had *so* much to give, and I always felt safe when I was with him. He could come across cold, but when it was just me and him, he was the warmest man I'd ever met. He was funny and caring, even if he didn't let everyone see that side of him. He wasn't a bad man. He didn't deserve what has happened to him."

Laura suddenly burst into tears and dropped her face into her hands. The priest walked forward and rested a hand on her shoulder as she sobbed in front of the crowd. Liz glanced awkwardly at Nancy, who was dabbing at the corners of her eyes with her fingers. Liz pulled out the packet of tissues and offered her friend one; she accepted it with a grateful smile.

When Laura finished her eulogy, she returned to the front row and sat next to Michael. He wrapped his arm around her, and she melted into his side. Liz could not imagine it was easy for him to hear her confess her love for another man considering their past.

"Do you think she's a good actress?" Nancy asked, stuffing the tissue into her pocket. "Because she convinced me."

"I don't know," Liz replied. "I don't feel right being here right now. I didn't know him."

"You found his body," Nancy replied quickly. "And you took in his dog. You've got as much right to be here as anyone."

Liz considered it for a moment, but she decided she was going to stick to her original plan, which had always been to leave before everyone else so she could question the one person she had been itching to speak to, but had not known how to get alone.

Liz stirred Paddy and shuffled along the row, whispering her apologies. She walked past the funeral car drivers and out of the church, suddenly feeling like she could not breathe.

Resting her hands on her knees, she looked down at the ground, her eyes closed. Something about Laura's speech had transported her back to a time she had tried to forget. Liz suddenly realised it was the first funeral she had attended since Lewis'.

"Are you okay, love?" one of the drivers asked. "Need a tissue?"

"I'm fine, thanks," Liz said, straightening up and pushing back the tears. "You know what funerals are like."

The man nodded his understanding before turning back to the church, leaving her to slip out of the grounds unseen. After dropping Paddy back at the flat and giving him an almost full bag of treats to devour, she set off to the place she had really wanted to visit today.

***

LIZ PUSHED THROUGH THE DOORS OF the Fish and Anchor, stunned by the silence that greeted her. She had not been wrong in assuming the entire town was currently at the church.

"You're early if you're here for the wake," Shirley, the tough and weathered landlady, said as she polished the bar. "I wish I could have gone to pay my respects, but that's the life of a landlady. Someone needs to hold the fort."

"He'd understand, I'm sure," Liz said with a smile. "I didn't know him too well myself, but I heard he liked it in here."

"I threw him out more than once, but I knew he didn't mean any harm by it," Shirley said firmly. "Aren't you the one who found Frank's body?"

"That was me," Liz said with an awkward smile. "And Adam's."

"Oh, right," Shirley said, nodding her recognition. "I thought it was. It's all such a blur. What are you? Some kind of medium or psychic?"

"I'm just a painter."

"I heard you were a detective," Shirley said with a sly smirk. "You hear a lot working here."

"A *retired* detective," Liz corrected her,

wondering if she should get it printed on a t-shirt considering how often she was asked the question. "That's what I wanted to talk to you about. I'm not here early by mistake."

"Pull up a stool," Shirley said. "What can I get you? I never discuss death without a drink. You look like a wine women to me. Can't stand the stuff personally, but I heard you were from the city."

"White wine, please," Liz said with a smile, deciding she liked Shirley. "Maybe you're the psychic one."

"Comes with the job, love," Shirley said as she poured a generous helping of wine into a glass. "On the house. Laura put some money behind the bar for everyone to get their first drink."

Shirley handed over the glass of wine before pouring herself a pint of bitter. She placed it on the bar to rest before leaning back to stare expectantly at Liz.

"How well would you say you knew Frank?" Liz asked.

"I thought you were retired?"

"I am."

"Then what's with the questions? You sound like

the police. Them lot have only just stopped poking around after someone bottled Adam. Not convinced the two things are connected."

"You're not?" Liz asked, pausing to sip the wine. "Why, if I can ask?"

"You can ask all you want, love," Shirley reached out for her dark pint. "Doesn't mean I'll answer."

"Like I said, I'm not police," Liz said. "Just a concerned citizen who can't seem to stop finding bodies."

"I like you," Shirley said after she sipped her pint, licking the foam off her lips. "I like a woman who isn't afraid to ask for what she wants. Frank and I go way back. We've known each other since school. It's a small place, but when you get to this age, there are fewer people that you've known for that long. Most move away, but recently we've been dropping like flies. You'd think we were in our eighties, not our fifties, but that's the way it is. It's usually cancer, not rat poison, but the end result is the same."

"So, you knew each other, but you weren't friends?"

"I liked him," she said. "He was honest, and he

didn't particularly like Mandy. We have that in common. Most useless barmaid I've ever hired, but she's pretty, and that counts for a lot in a fishing town full of old men. Laura had herself a good one there."

"I thought they split up before he died?" Liz said, repeating the rumour she had heard from Adam.

"Split up?" Shirley scoffed, shaking her head before sipping her drink again. "What makes you think that?"

"Mandy told Adam that she saw them arguing and Laura ran out crying."

Shirley rolled her eyes and wiped the foam from her mouth again. She rested the pint on the bar and leaned against the counter with her hands again.

"Typical Mandy," Shirley mumbled. "Complete bimbo, if you ask me. Jumps higher for a conclusion than a flea for a cat. I was here when that happened, but he wasn't breaking up with her."

"Why did she run out crying?"

"There's more than one thing that your fella can tell you to make you cry," Shirley said, clenching her jaw. "I probably shouldn't tell you. I overheard it, and then I spoke to Frank about it after Laura legged it."

"If it means anything, they're probably lowering Frank into the ground as we speak," Liz said, glancing at the clock behind the bar. "I don't think a dead man would mind you sharing his secrets."

"Let me just say this," Shirley said, leaning across the bar so that her face was inches from Liz's face. "Frank was heading for that grave with or without the rat poison."

Liz frowned as she let Shirley's words sink in.

"He was dying?"

"Pancreatic cancer," Shirley said bluntly. "I told you. Cancer usually gets people my age. I'll be next at this rate. Poor fella was a dead man walking. If someone wanted him dead so much, they should have just waited. He had months, if that. That's why I think he was suddenly drinking so much. He always liked a drink, but he had taken it to a new level. I think he wanted to go on his own terms, but he didn't have the guts to do it properly, probably for Laura's sake."

"And he definitely told Laura about this?"

"That's what I said, wasn't it?" Shirley snapped,

frowning down at Liz's wine. "Are you deaf?"

Liz smiled her apologies as she glanced back at the corner of the bar where she had seen Laura crying the day after Frank's death, and again with Michael on the day Adam died. Was her quick recovery down to her already having accepted Frank's imminent death?

"Whoever killed Frank can't have known about the cancer," Liz thought aloud. "That rules Laura out entirely. Did Mandy know?"

"If she did, she's kept it quiet," Shirley said before pouring the remains of her pint down the drain. "I try not to talk to her much. It's mainly hot air that comes out of her mouth. I'm sure her ears whistle when the sea breeze hits her right."

"Was she working here behind the bar when Adam died?" Liz asked, her mind racing.

"It was a busy day," Shirley said, arching a brow. "Football was on. I'm sure she was behind the bar, not that she's ever any use."

"I saw her sneaking out for a cigarette earlier that day," Liz said. "Did she sneak off again?"

"I've already told the police all of this," Shirley sighed with a roll of her eyes. "As far as I know, she went out to set the rat traps, and then I didn't see her leave again until she went out. That's when she screamed, and I ran out. You know the rest."

"And Adam?" Liz asked. "Did he come through the pub, or the back door?"

"Pub," Shirley replied abruptly, clearly growing annoyed by the newcomer's questioning. "He came in shouting the odds, saying he knew what had happened. That farmer boy took him out to the beer garden to calm him down. Farmer came back about thirty seconds later, and that's all I know.

"Simon?" Liz asked. "Are you sure? Did Adam mention who he thought killed Frank?"

"I've told you, the football was on," Shirley snapped. "People were cheering every bloody second. I couldn't hear myself think. Like I said, that's all I know. I need to get the food out of the kitchen before people get here. Can you move away from the bar? It's not a good look for when the funeral party arrives."

Liz nodded and slid off the stool, leaving her wine behind. She walked through to the eerily empty beer garden, which contrasted starkly with her first visit. Sitting on one of the benches, she tried to digest the new information she had heard.

She tried to think of the faces she had seen in the pub on the day of the football match, but half of Scarlet Cove had been there. Closing her eyes, she rubbed her temples on the side of her head and focussed. A face pushed forward in her mind, a face she had not considered until now, but suddenly felt so obvious. Liz jumped up and looked back into the pub, just as Mandy pushed on the door, followed by Laura. Liz now knew who had killed Frank and Adam, even if she did not have a scrap of evidence.

Fourteen

"Liz, I'm sorry. I'm really busy," Simon muttered as he rushed through the pub with a tray of cheese. "Shirley has put all of the cheese with the wrong crackers. I need to sort it out."

"But I need to tell you something," Liz pleaded. "It's important."

"Catch me later, okay?" he mumbled as he

rushed towards the food table.

After grabbing another glass of wine from the bar, which she had to pay for this time, she made her way over to Nancy, who was standing with her father and Jack, who were both playing on the fruit machine.

"Can I talk to you for a second?" Liz asked. "In private?"

Before Nancy could reply, Liz grabbed her arm and dragged her over to a quiet corner of the busy pub. Thankfully, most of the guests were gathered around the food table while Simon frantically sorted out the cheese.

"I *know* who killed Frank and Adam," she said. "I've figured it out."

"*How?*" Nancy responded with a dramatic gasp. "Are you sure?"

"I'm positive," Liz replied. "It all adds up. I don't know why I didn't see it before."

"Who is it?"

Liz leaned in and whispered the name into Nancy's ear. Just from the confused look on her friend's face, she knew nobody was going to believe her without evidence.

"But why –"

"Think about it," Liz said. "Really *think* about it."

Nancy grabbed Liz's wine and gulped down a generous amount of it before tapping her finger on her chin.

"I mean, I *could* almost understand Frank, but Adam too?"

"Adam was in here on the day he died," Liz said, taking back the wine and finishing it off. "He was shouting about knowing who killed Frank. They heard him and silenced him before he blew their cover in front of everyone."

"What are you going to do?" Nancy asked, her hand drifting up to her mouth. "Oh, Liz! Be careful."

"I'm going to call an old friend from Manchester," Liz said, pulling her phone from her handbag. "He'll know what the right procedure will be."

Nancy nodded before returning to her father and boyfriend. Liz scrolled to Miles' name in her phone, but she did not want to call him in the middle of the wake. She popped out to the beer garden, which was just as full as inside. Not wanting to leave the pub in case she saw the murderer, she slipped through the open door at the side of the bar and crept upstairs.

Shirley's flat above the pub was just as classically decorated as the downstairs. Fishing memorabilia lined the walls, and it did not look like it had been decorated in decades. She tiptoed along the creaky hallway towards the first room. It was a simply styled sitting room, which looked out over the market square.

Liz pressed the call button, pushing the phone against her ear. She realised it was the middle of the day and Miles was probably at work, but she hoped seeing her number was enough to make him pickup.

"Hello, stranger," Miles beamed down the phone. "How's the new life going?"

"It's *so good* to hear your voice," she sighed, letting the familiarity wash over her. "How's things?"

"Oh, you know," Miles said, the sound of shuffling papers in the background. "Busy. Your replacement doesn't hold a candle to you. Calling to tell me you've realised you've made a huge mistake?"

"No, but I've called you to tell you that you

were right," she said, walking over to the window, and pulling back the net curtains. "It's crazy here. Two murders already, and I wasn't expecting any."

"Two?" Miles cried. "Bloody hell, Liz. I thought you were starting a new peaceful life by the sea?"

"I am."

"Sounds like you've moved to the Middle East," he mocked, the shuffling growing louder. "What do you want? I'm guessing this isn't a social call."

"I need your advice," she confessed, stepping back from the window to cast her eyes over the trinkets on top of the fireplace. "I think I've figured out who the murderer is, but the local police are next to useless. Wouldn't know how to conduct a murder investigation if the murderer walked into the station covered in blood with a signed confession pinned to their chest."

"Sounds about right for those small places," Miles said, followed by heavy slurping. "We're up to our eyeballs here, but I've always got time for you. What advice do you need?"

"I have no evidence," she said. "Nothing concrete. I just have a feeling. I haven't even told the police yet. I only figured it out today. What do I do,

Miles?"

"With no evidence?" Miles laughed down the phone. "You do nothing, and you leave it alone. You're retired."

"But I have a hunch."

"And your hunches are always right, but how would you have liked it if a busy body started sticking their nose into one of your cases."

"I wouldn't," Liz mumbled, suddenly feeling a little foolish. "But they've already killed twice and –"

The sound of smashing glass broke her off mid-sentence. She held her breath and listened out, sure the noise had been too close to have come from downstairs.

"Liz?" Miles called down the phone. "Are you still there?"

"I'll call you back," she muttered, before immediately hanging up and dropping the phone back into her bag.

Liz crept carefully along the sitting room floor, every floorboard squeaking underfoot. She opened the door, its hinges in serious need of oiling. She listened out, hoping something else would smash. When it did not, she wondered if the sound had travelled from the pub after all. She almost headed back downstairs, none the wiser on what she should do, until she heard a women's mumbled voice.

Liz walked to the end of the hall towards a slightly ajar door. She listened for a second, the sound of mumbling growing more irritated by the second. Liz almost knocked, until she heard a man's voice huff something inaudible.

Without a second thought, Liz pushed on the door, shocked to see Michael pinning Laura up against the wall, his mouth against hers. Liz almost stepped back again, until she saw Laura's wide and afraid stare. The two women met each other's gazes, and Laura's moans, which Liz realised were cries for help, grew stronger.

Liz darted forward and dragged Michael off the tiny woman. He fell back onto the bed, his lips bright red.

"What are you doing?" he cried, his voice gruff. "She's my wife!"

"Laura, are you okay?" Liz asked.

She nodded, but she did not look okay. After wiping her mouth, she panted for breath before she began crying. Michael stood up and put his hand out towards her, but Liz batted it away and stepped between them.

"Fifteen years in the Greater Manchester Police, pal," Liz said, her old commanding tone back in an instant. "I've fought bigger and scarier, and won, so I suggest you step back if you know what's good for you."

"I said, she's my *wife*," he repeated, his eyes darkening.

"We're not together, Michael," Laura called from behind Liz's shoulder. "And we never will be. We're just friends now."

"I don't think you'll want to be even that, Laura," Liz said, stepping back, so she had them both in her view. "I'm sorry to say this, but your husband killed Frank and Adam."

"*W-what?*" Laura cried, laughing through her tears. "No, he didn't."

"Yes, he did," Liz said firmly, turning to Michael. "I never even suspected you until today. Not until I realised that Frank was dying and Michael would have had no idea."

The look of surprise in Michael's eyes told Liz everything she needed to know; she had been right.

"Are you going to listen to this, Laura?" Michael demanded. "Who is this idiot, anyway?"

"She's the new woman," Laura mumbled, her eyes narrowed on Liz. "She used to be a detective."

"That's right," Liz said. "And I'm pretty ashamed to say it took me this long. Michael's name kept popping up. You had the perfect motive to kill Frank."

"To steal his fish?" Michael mocked.

"No," Liz said, turning to Laura with a sad smile. "You wanted your wife back. You were tired of seeing another man with the woman you loved, so you plotted to get him out of the way so you could claim Laura for yourself again."

"I would never have taken you back," Laura mocked, her lips twisted. "You were an awful husband. You didn't care about me, or what I wanted, you just wanted to keep me like a pet. The only reason I stayed friends with you was because I was scared of how you'd react if I dared cut ties."

"I love you," Michael mumbled. "I did it because I love you."

A lump rose in Liz's throat. She slipped her hand into her bag, gripped her phone, unlocked it, and opened the voice recorder app.

"The night Christopher came in here to humiliate Frank and take his flask away after hearing about his drinking, you saw your chance." Liz paused and looked down to make sure the phone was recording. "You went to the office before you knew Frank would start. You saw the rat poison, and you put some in his hip flask, knowing the drunk would take it back the first chance he got."

"Frank wasn't a drunk," Laura jumped in, her anger directed at Liz. "He was sick. He was dying. He drank to numb the pain because he didn't want to think about it."

"I bet you were rubbing your hands together when everyone thought Frank died by accident, weren't you?" Liz asked, staring deep into Michael's eyes. "You just needed to wait until Laura ran back into your arms. That was until Adam figured out it was you, so you killed him too."

"Why, Michael?" Laura cried. "He was just a boy."

"He figured it out!" Michael cried, spitting as he snarled. "He saw me that morning in the office. I lied my way through and said I was looking for money to steal. I thought it would be better than going to prison for murder, but the kid kept his mouth shut for that one. He'd still be alive now if he'd just kept his mouth shut properly, but when he heard Frank was poisoned, he put two and two together and –"

"Got four?" Liz jumped in.

"Took him a few days to connect the dots," Michael said. "He ran in here shouting about knowing who killed Frank the second he figured it out. He should have just gone straight to the police, but he was dense. I followed him outside. I still had my bottle of beer in my hand, so I did what I needed to. I noticed the cameras pointing right at me, so I slipped into the back of the pub. The football kept Shirley distracted. This place still records on VHS, the fools. It was as simple as taking the tape and putting in a clean one. I tossed the thing out to sea after making sure to destroy the film."

"Michael," Laura said, choking back the tears. "I don't know who you are anymore."

"I'm your husband."

"*No,*" she whispered. "The man I married would never have done this."

"I did it for *us*!" he cried, his voice booming. "I did it because we deserved a fresh start."

"No, Michael," Liz jumped in, taking a step forward. "You did it for you. Don't put that on Laura. She had every right to leave you for a man who treated her better. She wasn't your possession."

"We can still be happy," Michael cried, stepping forward and grabbing Laura's hands tightly in his. "Nobody else knows. We can sort this."

Liz knew exactly what he meant, but she was not scared of him. She would fight him to the death if she had to, as long as someone heard the recording.

"Michael, you're not well," Laura sobbed, tears tumbling silently down her cheeks. "You need help."

"*No!*" he cried, pulling Laura into a tight embrace. "I just need you!"

Liz tried to pull him off, but the back of his hand struck Liz across the face. She tumbled to the floor, the contents of her bag flying everywhere. Her phone slid across the floor, stopping by Michael's foot.

"You're recording me?" he cried, letting go of Laura to turn to Liz. "Why would you do that?"

Michael stamped his foot down on the phone,

cracking the screen just as Miles' picture popped up as he attempted to call her. Michael reached into the back of his jeans and pulled out a pocketknife. With a sharp flick, the glittering blade popped up.

"I knew it would only be a matter of time until someone else figured it out," he said, a manic smile spreading across his face as he walked forward, kicking the phone out of the way. "I knew I had to be better prepared than I was with Adam."

Liz looked around the room for something she could throw at Michael, but nothing was in reach. She thought about scrambling away or jumping up, but she knew she could do neither fast enough to evade the blade. Liz gulped and closed her eyes for a moment. She thought about Lewis, her husband's face calming her. If this were really the end, at least they would be together soon.

Just as Liz was about to accept her fate, there was a loud crack, followed by a heavy thud. Liz opened her eyes, first seeing Laura holding a large marble candlestick over her head, and then seeing Michael slumped lifelessly on the ground, the knife inches from his hand. Liz sprung up and grabbed the knife, and Laura dropped the candlestick with a heavy thump. They stared at each other for a moment, before Laura crumpled against the chest of drawers from which she had grabbed the candlestick. She sobbed into her hands.

"This is *all* my fault," Laura sobbed. "Frank died because of me and poor Adam, he was so young. I was going to tell Michael about Frank's cancer, but I didn't want him to get his hopes up."

"None of this is your fault, Laura," Liz said softly. "You didn't know Michael was capable of this."

"What are we going to do? If Michael is dead, his story is dead with him. He was right about one thing when he said no one will believe us."

"That isn't quite correct," a voice came from the door as it pushed open. Mandy stepped inside, clutching a microphone in her hands. "I was in the bathroom going over my speech when I heard shouting. I came over and listened for a second and when I heard what was happening, I turned this thing on. I don't really know how it works, but I think everyone downstairs heard enough to testify if they have to."

Liz stepped over Michael's body, just as she

heard multiple sets of footsteps rushing up the stairs.

"Sounds like it worked," Liz exclaimed. "Mandy, I could kiss you!"

Shirley appeared behind Mandy, followed by Simon, Christopher, Nancy, Jack, Tim, and a dozen other customers.

"We couldn't figure out where it was coming from!" Shirley cried. "We heard everything!"

"*Liz*!" Nancy cried, pushing through the crowd and hurrying into the room before grabbing Liz in the tightest hug yet. "We've called the police! I can't believe you faced him like that. I think you're my hero."

Liz smiled over Nancy's shoulder as Simon pushed through the crowd, his face white as he stared down at Michael as he began to stir.

"Mind if I step in?" Simon asked sheepishly.

Nancy smiled and moved away without argument. Simon did not wait for Liz to reply. He snaked his arms around her and hugged her so tight, she was sure she was going to pop. She did not mind though. She leaned into the hug, feeling the safest she had done all day. She closed her eyes and let the seriousness of the situation wash over her as butterflies danced in her stomach. When she opened her eyes, she met Christopher's as he smiled sadly at them. She pulled away from the hug, but Christopher turned and walked back down the stairs.

"I should have listened to you before," Simon said with a soft smile, brushing Liz's fallen strands behind her ears. "I was too distracted by cheese."

Michael let out a huge groan as Jack tied his hands behind his back with his belt.

"At least he's not dead," Nancy announced as she helped Laura up off the floor. "I would never have guessed it was Michael. I didn't even believe you when you said you thought it was him."

"I don't think any of us believed it," Liz said, looking around at all of the eyes staring at her. "If fifteen years in the force taught me anything, it's that you should expect the unexpected, and never be afraid to call for backup."

As if on cue, police sirens moved in from the distance. Shirley walked into the room and wrapped her arm around Mandy, who had been staring at Michael since opening the door. For the first time since Frank's death, Liz saw Mandy's veneer crack, and she began to cry.

"I think we all deserve a stiff drink," Liz announced to a sea of nods. "The first round is on me."

Fifteen

Michael's public confession and arrest was all people could talk about in the following days, which gave Liz plenty of time to put the finishing touches to her shop.

On the morning of the grand opening, Liz found herself in Crazy Waves, fiddling with her hair in the mirror.

"I couldn't believe it when I heard him over the

speakers," Polly said, curling another piece of Liz's fiery hair around a hot barrel. "I thought I was being contacted by the other side. I'm a little bit psychic you know. On my mum's side, but I definitely have the sight. You can't trust anyone these days."

"I guess not," Liz said absently, having already completely exhausted the conversation with every person she had come into contact with. "I'm just ready to get the shop open and start a new chapter."

"Well, you look stunning, babe," Polly announced in her usual squeaky tone. "My work is done."

Liz did not recognise herself as she looked in the mirror, which she was sure would happen every time she stepped into Polly's salon. In place of her usual frizz were glamorous, wavy curls, which cascaded softly down her face.

"Who are you and what have you done with Liz," Nancy gushed when Liz walked out of the salon. "C'mon. Let's go and find something in that wardrobe of yours to match this hair."

Once back at Liz's flat, Nancy dug through all of Liz's clothes, disregarding the majority of them by throwing them dramatically over her head and onto the growing pile on Liz's bed.

"What about this?" Nancy exclaimed, holding up an off-the-shoulder number, which flared out at the waist with deep purple and blue swirls that made her red hair stand out. "You'd look so pretty in this."

"I wore that on my final date with Lewis," Liz remembered aloud, her heart swelling. "It's perfect."

"Who's Lewis?" Nancy asked as she handed over the dress.

"A story for another day," Liz said, accepting the dress before shooing Nancy out of the bedroom.

Liz slipped into the dress, and despite not having worn it for two years, it fit her like a glove. She assessed her reflection in the mirror after slipping into a pair of heels she had borrowed from Nancy after finding out they had the same size feet. She barely recognised herself. She was not sure that she looked like an artist, but she did look like a business owner who was ready to show the world her dream.

"You scrub up well," Nancy exclaimed when Liz slipped out of the room. "You look beautiful!"

"It's not too much, is it?" Liz said.

"It's perfect," Nancy assured her. "And it's certain to turn a special someone's head."

"I don't know who you mean," Liz replied with a wink. "Are there many people out there?"

"Oh, a few," Nancy mumbled, her cheeks blushing as she headed to the door. "You ready?"

"I think so," she said, checking herself one last time before spritzing some perfume on her neck and wrists, something she rarely remembered to do. "This is what I came to Scarlet Cove to do, so let's do it."

Nancy opened the door to Liz's flat and hurried down to the door at the bottom of the stairs. Liz followed her down, the rumble of the crowd much louder than she had anticipated.

"How many people are out there?" she asked.

Instead of answering, Nancy opened the door, the bright sun blinding Liz. She shielded her eyes with her hand, shocked to see a sea of faces gathered in front of her tiny shop.

"Oh my –,"

"I forgot to tell you," Nancy said, pulling the newspaper out of her bag. "You're the front page news this morning, and they mentioned your opening. I made sure to mention it when I spoke to the reporters."

Liz took the newspaper and looked at the headline, which read '*NEWCOMER CATCHES KILLER*', next to pictures of Frank, Adam, Michael, and one of her old police headshots. Laughing to herself, she passed the newspaper back to Nancy and looked back at the crowd, catching Simon's eyes. He began to clap, then applause spread quickly through the crowd of familiar faces, who were all smiling at her. She spotted Katelyn standing next to Christopher at the back of the crowd; her steely expression and folded arms stuck out like a sore thumb.

"For the paper," a young man with a large camera said, jumping in front of Liz.

She smiled back uneasily at the camera lens as Nancy passed her a huge pair of golden scissors.

"Would you care to do the honours, Elizabeth Jones," the photographer shouted over the chattering crowd. "Nice big smile when you do."

Liz shuffled to the front of the crowd, never in her wildest dreams having imagined there would be this much interest in her tiny arts and crafts shop. She knew they were there because she was Scarlet Cove's current hot topic, but she did not care if they were going to buy something. She just hoped she had ordered enough stock.

Swallowing her nerves, Liz smiled down the camera lens and snipped the red ribbon with one swift chop. The camera flashed over and over as the crowd cheered.

"I declare Blank Canvas open!" Liz exclaimed as she tossed open the door, glancing up at the hand-painted sign above the window. "Let's get this party started!"

It did not take long for Liz's shop to fill up, and she was happy to see that people were putting things in their basket while Nancy worked behind the till.

"Surprise," a familiar voice whispered in her ear as he placed his hands over her eyes.

"*Miles!*" she cried, turning and wrapping her arms around him. "I'm so glad to see you. What are you doing here?"

"I needed to see you were in one piece after that phone call," he whispered into her ear as he squeezed tight. "You made the national news. It's all people are talking about back home. Once a detective, always a detective, right?"

"*Retired* detective," she reminded him.

"Officially, now. I'm done with murder investigations."

"For now," he said with a wink. "You've got yourself a nice setup here. This place looks like it's good for you."

"It is," Liz said, exhaling heavily. "It really is."

"Have you told anyone yet?"

"Not yet," she said, knowing he was referring to Lewis. "Maybe I will one day, maybe I won't. I'll see."

Miles pinched her cheek before floating away, following a tray of cheese nibbles, which was being carried by one of the waitresses she had hired specially.

Her friend from back home was replaced almost instantly by Christopher, who was clutching a large gift-wrapped square in his hands.

"Congratulations," he said, smiling awkwardly. "I got this for you. It's just a little something."

Liz tore back the brown paper, surprised to see a detailed painting of Scarlet Cove in a chunky gold frame. She could see the castle and the harbour, tiny boats out at sea, and a tiny redheaded figure painting on the beach.

"Where did you get this?"

"Katelyn has some contacts," he said. "I had them paint it especially for you. That's you, painting, in a painting. I'm not much of an art buff, but Katelyn said it was technically good."

"I don't know what to say," Liz said, staring dumbfounded down at the picture. "Thank you, Christopher. It's so thoughtful."

"I can't stay," he said, before coughing into his fist and glancing over at his sister, who was lingering by the door and looking down her nose into a basket of children's paints. "I have a business meeting. I just wanted to come and wish you luck."

Christopher held out his hand, and Liz gratefully accepted it. She knew it meant that he did not mind that she did not want to date him officially, and that they were going to continue as friends.

Liz showed the painting to Nancy before hanging it proudly on the wall next to the storeroom door so that everyone who walked up to the counter would see it. Grabbing Paddy from Jack, Liz pushed through the waiters in the storeroom and out into the yard.

When she was finally alone, she leaned her head against the outside of the building and exhaled heavily, unable to believe she had pulled it off.

"Penny for your thoughts?" Simon asked as he slipped out of the shop. "I saw you leave. Why are you not enjoying your party? You're the woman of the hour."

"Paddy needed the bathroom," she said with a smile. "And I think I needed a moment to soak everything in."

"Have you tried the cheese yet?" he asked, pushing forward the tray he was holding. "When you asked me to cater your opening, I thought long and hard about what cheese would suit you."

"Oh?"

"A pepper jack Red Leicester," he said, pointing out the tiny flecks of red in the orange cheese. "A little sweet, a little spicy, and very sharp."

"I'm flattered."

"Here," Simon lifted up one of the pieces of cracker from the tray and guided it to her mouth. "I think you'll like it."

Instead of letting her take it from him, he fed it to her, his fingers brushing softly against her lips as a nervous smile spread across his blushing face.

"It's really good," she mumbled through the mouthful. "Oh, and *there's* the spice."

He chuckled like a schoolboy before tossing one down to Paddy, who caught it with an expert bite. In his white shirt and bowtie, and with his golden hair gelled back, Simon looked more handsome than ever, and she was no longer afraid to admit that to herself.

"Have I told you how beautiful you look yet?" he said, his voice husky and soothing. "Because you do."

Liz parted her lips to speak, but she did not know what to say. Simon edged closer, his dazzling eyes locking with hers. Butterflies circled in her stomach, letting her know this was what she wanted. She closed her eyes and waited for Simon's lips to brush against hers, but Paddy's loud bark separated them.

They both laughed awkwardly for a moment as Liz's face turned as bright red as Simon's. She crouched down and scratched behind Paddy's ears, the moment gone.

"I should get back," he said, pulling on the door.

"The cheese won't hand itself out."

Liz nodded her understanding and waited for Simon to slip back inside before leaning against the wall and exhaling once more, but for a different reason. The door opened again, and Liz jumped up, expecting to see Simon, a little disappointed to see Nancy.

"There you are," Nancy said breathlessly. "We're out of bags, and I don't know which box to look in. Oh, Liz. You're bright red. Is everything okay?"

"Everything is fine," Liz said, meaning every word. "Everything is completely fine. C'mon, I'll show you."

Liz walked back into the storeroom and dodged past one of the waiters to grab a fresh box of plastic bags. She followed Nancy back into the shop, and it somehow looked even busier than before.

Liz caught Simon's gaze in the crowd, and they shared a warm smile for a moment. She decided she was going to enjoy her new life in Scarlet Cove very much indeed.

If you enjoyed *Dead in the Water*, why not sign up to Agatha Frost and Evelyn Amber's **free** newsletters at **AgathaFrost.com** and **EvelynAmber.com** to hear about brand new releases!

Coming October 2017! Liz and friends are back for another Scarlet Cove case in *Castle on the Hill!*

24388648R00143

Printed in Poland
by Amazon Fulfillment
Poland Sp. z o.o., Wrocław